Relative Trutn

A Miscarriage of Justice and a Barrister's
Journey to Right that Wrong

by

Caroline Walker

Fortis Publishing Services

ISBN-13: 978-1-913822-25-5

Fortis Publishing
Kemp House
160 City Road
London
EC1V 2NX

This book is inspired by a true story, a story the author was directly involved in.
All major events happened, although names and locations have been changed and some scenes fictionalised.
The main characters are seeded from real people.

"It takes a village to raise a child..."

African Proverb

Acknowledgments

I'd like to thank all those who have helped me write this book.

Particularly 'my village' of family and friends and colleagues who guided me and inspired me to be the best and to fight for justice.

About the Author

Caroline Walker was bought up by her father in South London and attended the worst school in her area.

Thereafter, she worked in Italy, London and the Caribbean, but her travels ended with the birth of her child.

Caroline embraced the life change with ease and lived in hope that the father of her child would take on parental responsibilities as she had. However, this was not to be, and her situation went from bad to worse. She fought against the odds to bring some normality and structure into her life as a single parent.

Unfortunately, Caroline developed a condition that led to an unusual chain of events and a major change in career. She became a barrister. It was this journey, with life's ups and downs, that brought her back into a relationship with the father of her child, one that took unexpected twists and turns.

TO MY SONS

you continue to inspire me

FOREWORD

Having read the book, I find the author's true story both astonishing and gripping. She has a unique attitude for someone having gone through and been confronted by such a life experience. This is exactly the type of individual this profession needs 'Fighters for Justice and Equal treatment.'

This is truly a treasure account. In a word, stunning.

Dr. Courtenay Griffiths K.C.

1

THE HEIST

It was by far his biggest job to date, more serious than any drug deal. It didn't compare to a little protection or roughing someone up because they hadn't paid their debts. This was big time, a premeditated, armed robbery with real guns. And there was more. The plan was to fire a gun, not intending to kill or maim, just a threat.

Cooper, a nickname his mates had christened him with years ago, knew that most people buckled under threat as long as the warning was real and could be backed up with force if necessary. And he could manage that; he was an intimidating sight, all six feet of him with the physique of a pro cage fighter.

Dressed in designer clothes, he presented himself well with the look that ladies liked. From the fifteen grand Rolex watches, Gucci suits, and jackets to the Burberry leather brogues; he had it all. When casual, he preferred Stone Island jeans. He bore a passing resemblance to the up-and-coming actor, Idris Elba.

The Mossberg 500 pump-action shotgun was Cooper's weapon of choice that day. He had never used or fired one before and he couldn't shake the feeling that he was stepping into unknown territory. For the first time in his life, he was nervous; worried even. Armed robbery carried a fifteen-year sentence, but Cooper, being the designated shooter, faced the more serious charge of aggravated armed robbery; a twenty-five-year stretch if it all went pear-shaped.

He tried not to think about it and told himself he was a professional. The planning, and, in particular, his own additional preparation, had been meticulous. He had bought the sawn-off shotgun from a pal in Whitechapel. He knew him well. The gun was untraceable. His mate was a diamond, an old school felon who knew how to keep his mouth shut no matter how much heat they put on him.

The plan was a simple one. He had been watching a particular jeweller's store on New Bond Street for some weeks. Cooper told himself Asprey Jewellers deserved to be robbed. The security was almost non-existent. A switch behind the counter controlled the lock on the door and two CCTV cameras covered part of the entrance and immediately inside. It was a joke. The shop was one of the busiest on the street with a regular flow of clientele from around ten in the morning through to close of day at five-thirty. The busiest time was between one and two o'clock. Cooper had chosen one-thirty to make the hit to be sure they got inside as a customer left; there was no way the shop assistant would activate the door to allow three masked men into the premises.

Balaclavas and ski masks were a must because of CCTV; the curse of the criminal classes. More and more were being deployed around London. It was 1994; Cooper figured that in another ten years the capital would be saturated with them. But not today in New Bond Street.

Cooper had pinpointed every CCTV camera in the immediate vicinity. The Armani store, Mulberry, and Barclays Bank. There was a camera on the corner of Brook Street and at the crossroads of Maddox Street. No more. It wouldn't be difficult to act normal; window shop the designer stores. They would keep out of range of the cameras and, when they got closer to Asprey Jewellers, pull on the masks.

Cooper left his apartment at noon; his two associates, Harry O'Connell and Leroy Stanley, left from different addresses at the same time in Clapham and Dulwich Village. For once, Cooper had dressed down. He wore sunglasses and a baseball cap, a pair of black jeans, Cuban heel boots and a black sweatshirt hoody, sporting the name of an American University. He carried a rucksack that contained the shotgun, balaclava, a black lightweight bomber jacket and a pay-as-you-go Motorola mobile phone. Apart from a little money, he had nothing else.

Taking the Victoria Line to Green Park Station, he checked the time. He controlled his breathing and limited the number of times he looked at his watch. As arranged, texts announced the other two members of the team were on route; everything was on schedule.

As he walked along Piccadilly towards Old Bond Street, he glanced at the time.

Far too early, he thought to himself. *No worries, better than being late.*

He stopped at a few shops, called into a bookstore, and browsed the biographies. At one-thirteen, another two texts, both men were now on New Bond Street; it was all systems go. They had studied the police activity there; it was sporadic with no timed patrols. Some days there was hardly a copper in sight. But they couldn't take that chance today. There would be no patrols on New Bond Street as Asprey Jewellers was being robbed, not a copper nearby. Cooper had made sure of that.

* * *

It was what he called smart thinking. He was the brains behind the entire operation, with an above-average intelligence and a little cunning planning. He had paid two men 500 quid to cause a ruckus in a pub a few streets away. They would keep their mouths shut.

Cooper loved to fight. He mixed in circles with other like-minded individuals. The Slug and Lettuce on Hanover Street was a known Chelsea football fans' pub; the notorious Chelsea hooligan firm, the Headhunters, met there for a few beers on match days. His mates were from a rival firm, the Millwall Bushwackers. Persuading them to storm the pub for a tear up hadn't been hard to do. Amassing a small army of around twenty-five hooligans, they had planned a military-style operation.

After the altercation, the Bushwackers would have a tidy sum to spend on drink back in The Duke; safe territory in the Isle of Dogs. Cooper had been crafty. He told them he had bumped into the Headhunters on a night out in London. There was a strong National Front element in the firm and he'd told the Millwall boys that the rival gang had picked on him and given him a good kicking. It was payback time. Cooper wanted the pub smashed up and as many of the Headhunters as possible beaten to a pulp. The instructions had been simple. Storm the pub at one o'clock and cause as much mayhem as possible.

He heard the first police siren at exactly one-seventeen. A smile pulled across his face as he imagined the carnage in the pub. Perfect.

* * *

Cooper waited a few minutes and checked his watch again. He adjusted his baseball cap further down over his forehead and fumbled in his rucksack. He pulled out the black jacket, put it on, and zipped it up before striding in the target's direction.

As the last two texts arrived, he passed Tiffany and Co. It was one-twenty-nine. O'Connell loitered twenty yards from Asprey's doorway out of range of the CCTV cameras while Stanley looked in a shop window. They were ready and in position. Now it was just a matter of being patient.

At one-thirty-three, his eyes fixed on O'Connell sprinting towards the doorway of Asprey's; Cooper took off after him, focusing on the door of the shop. Stanley turned and ran across the road. Their masks were on as they came into range of the shop cameras. A young couple, who had purchased a Kindrea, white-gold, diamond engagement ring, froze as O'Connell jammed his foot in the open doorway and hustled them back into the shop. He held the door open for Cooper and Stanley, who were a split second behind him.

Cooper reached into his rucksack and pulled out the shotgun; terror covered the faces of the three assistants. He wasn't taking any chances; the sole male assistant looked the 'have a go hero' type, but the colour drained from the middle-aged man's face as Cooper pumped and cocked the shotgun. He pointed it at the ceiling and fired once. As the shotgun pellets embedded in the ceiling, a fine white plaster cloud drifted gently downwards.

"Do as I say," Cooper ordered, "and you'll all be

fine."

It was like taking candy from a baby. The shotgun blast had had the desired effect. The three assistants unlocked the display cases where Rolex and Brequet watches lay; diamond and gold rings, necklaces and bracelets sparkled. Even that part of the heist had been well planned; they were only to take items that could be carried in three rucksacks and easily offloaded onto their contacts and fences. Cooper had told the other two not to be greedy, not to hang around the store too long. There were silent alarms in London's jeweller's shops; he knew that the chance of an assistant activating one of them was pretty high.

He focused on the second hand of his watch while the assistants dropped watches, bracelets, necklaces, and rings into the open rucksacks. He had allowed exactly three minutes in the shop.

"Fifteen seconds," he said.

Stanley turned around to face him. "Fuck that. Give us another few minutes here and we'll clean up."

Cooper growled. "Ten fucking seconds."

"But—"

"Nine... eight... seven... "

Stanley and O'Connell loaded another dozen watches into the rucksacks before Cooper gave the signal to go. They knew better than to argue with him and walked from the store, still masked up.

Stanley headed north along New Bond Street and, when he was safely out of view of the cameras, he removed his mask. O'Connell headed south and did the same. Cooper walked across the road, still wearing his mask. The people of London barely gave him a second glance; no people-watchers there. When he was halfway down one of the many alleys in that part of London and sure he was alone, he removed the mask and stuffed it into his rucksack. At the bottom of the road, he jumped on a bus pulling away from a stop. He sat on the back seat and let out a sigh. The faint sound of police sirens filtered through an open window. They would be en route to Asprey Jewellers. They were too late.

Another two texts four minutes later to say the boys were safely on London transport. They would meet up the following day at noon.

Their haul was a decent one. They calculated around 750 thousand quid on the black market. It would take some time; they wouldn't rush into offloading the stolen goods. Cooper had ordered them to sit tight for two months.

2

SUSPICION

The police had nothing to go on. Apart from the footage from the shop's CCTV, there was nothing else: no witnesses, no fingerprints, no DNA. The male assistant described them as 'just normal guys' but somehow he was convinced two were black and one was white.

However, there was one grain of hope offered by the young female shop assistant about the man with the shotgun. She had kept her eyes on the shooter who had fired into the ceiling. She described him as being built like a rugby player, possibly six two or three; his eyes were full of malice and bloodshot. Cold, like the devil's. And even though he was wearing a mask, she somehow sensed that he was handsome.

In his mid-50s, DI Dave Graham led the case. He ran his hand through his greying hair as he leaned his well-toned frame against a filing cabinet next to his desk. He couldn't quite understand her observation. He had wanted to get hold of the stupid cow and give her a shake.

How the fuck could she have known that? he thought.

She had told him that the shooter's voice was distinctive and menacing.

"Would you know it again if he stood in front of you and spoke?" he'd asked.

"I don't think so," she'd replied.

DI Graham played out the conversation in his head and then let out a sigh, looked over at his colleague, and pointed to the PC monitor.

"Let's have another look at the first CCTV from the shop. Perhaps we've missed something."

* * *

Gary Jackson had celebrated his forty-eighth birthday in an upmarket restaurant. For years he had been a small-time petty criminal who looked after himself and no one else. He tended not to get his hands dirty these days and liked to think he was smart. He didn't burgle houses anymore and refused to get involved in anything to do with drugs. He was a specialist, or so he thought. Although he dressed smart but casual, the outside world wouldn't have thought Jackson made a decent living moving things on; his appearance belied his true worth.

In the early days, he would have taken anything from a stolen TV to a microwave, a moped, or a laptop. But he quickly realised there was no point in risking the long arm of the law to turnover a fifty or sixty-pound profit. He had edged up the scale; high-value cars, BMWs, Mercedes, and Range Rovers, where a five-minute phone call could make him six or seven grand. And jewellery too; rings, necklaces, bracelets, earrings, and brooches, but especially watches. He had become quite the watch expert. He loved watches, especially Rolex and again, just like with a top-of-the-range Merc, a decent Rolex watch would make him a tidy sum simply by moving it on to one of the many bent dealers he knew around London and the Home Counties.

Jackson had another trade. He was a police informer, a coppers nark, a snitch.

It had been three months since the armed raid on Asprey Jewellers and there had been no arrests. But DI Graham knew that items from the raid were now in circulation and he needed results. He especially wanted to take down the shooter.

Graham met Jackson, the Watch Man, in a pub basement in London's West End. It was cool and trendy, more wine sold than beer, packed full of the city type: traders, bankers, entrepreneurs, and lawyers.

It was a perfect location. The conversation

wouldn't take long, it never did. The two men blended into the background, tucked away in a dark corner where you could barely see the shape of your glass. It wasn't healthy mixing with the likes of Jackson. Jackson felt the same about Graham. If any of his contacts ever saw him with a well-known copper, his cover would be blown and a professional hit would no doubt be actioned within days.

"I just need a name." Graham started on his third pint of the day.

Jackson seemed reluctant... nervous. "You haven't given me anything for over a year now. You know I could put you away for a ten stretch as easy as that." Graham snapped his fingers.

And Jackson knew he could. Graham was a bastard and well known for getting results. He knew how to manipulate those in power. It was rumoured that he had tampered with evidence on many occasions.

"Just one name," he repeated. "Nothing else, no addresses, no evidence, nada."

"You don't need a watch?" Jackson asked.

Graham shook his head.

"If we take a watch in evidence, then it will compromise you."

Jackson sighed and wiped the sweat from his brow.

"Corey, Lee Corey."

Graham raised an eyebrow. "You sure?"

"One hundred fucking percent, the shit has come

from him. I've moved about thirty grand on just by myself. He's a man on a mission."

Well, I'll be fucked. The detective's head swirled.

"And there's one other thing," Jackson said.

"What's that?"

"Well, I shouldn't really tell you, but... "

"Go on."

"I've heard on good authority that Corey was in the market for a shotgun a few months ago."

"You think he was the shooter?" the detective questioned.

Jackson didn't bother to reply. There was no need to.

Graham didn't finish his beer; he didn't even thank his snitch. After climbing the few steps to the street, he walked out into the dull London day. It all fell into place. The female assistant from Asprey's, the description, six foot two and built like a rugby player, handsome under the mask. Evil eyes and a distinctive voice. She'd described Corey to a tee.

Graham held out his hand at a passing cab. It braked quickly and swerved across the road, much to the annoyance of the woman in the car behind.

"Where to, Guv'nor?" the cabby asked.

Graham told him. The cabby was one of the annoying types who insisted on striking up a conversation. A cheery chap who loved his job.

"Having a good day, Guv?"

He ignored the cabby. The man got the message when Graham pulled out his phone. He sent a text to his colleague back at the station.

I'll be there in twenty, need to pull in Corey for Asprey job.

* * *

Thirty-five-year-old DI Holland eased his stocky frame into the chair opposite his colleague in West End Central. Graham never disclosed his sources, but confirmed that the tip-off was sound. This impressed Holland.

"Corey has offloaded the goods; he has lain low for a while but now he wants his return."

"We need a warrant," Holland replied.

Graham nodded over the cup of coffee he cupped in both hands.

"No problem, as sure as eggs are eggs, we'll get the warrant and he'll have some of that shit in his gaff."

They executed the raid forty-eight hours later. Corey was more than useful in a fight, so Graham had taken along half a dozen of the hardest bastards on the force. It disappointed Holland that Corey hadn't resisted. He enjoyed that side of the job; it got the adrenalin pumping and a chance to roll around the floor. But something didn't feel right. Corey was too calm, as if he'd been expecting the raid. He sat at the kitchen table and told the police team to fill their boots as he settled down with a black coffee and read that day's *London Evening Standard*. Graham sat opposite, uninvited, and poured himself a coffee from the cafetière on the table. Corey smiled.

"We know it was you, Lee. We know you were the shooter."

"No comment," Corey said.

"And we'll prove it one way or another."

"No comment."

"We'll find one of those watches somewhere," he pointed back through to the lounge. "In there, in a bedroom, under a floorboard, or even in your car. We'll rip the fucking thing to pieces, strip it down to the bare metal and we'll find something."

"No comment."

"And the shop assistant says she could point you out, says she would recognise your voice. It was distinctive."

"No comment."

They took two black sacks of clothing away from Corey's flat. Four pairs of jeans and sweatshirts, three hoodies, a black jumper, a waterproof jerkin, a bomber jacket and three pairs of trainers. They even removed eight pairs of socks, a scarf and three pairs of gloves. Graham was counting on gunshot residue from when the shooter had fired the gun into the ceiling. How a jury just loved gunshot residue. It wasn't as if the police could plant that sort of thing. Any test results would come from the outside independent body they regularly employed; it was foolproof. They had found nothing to link Corey to the actual robbery. It was now up to the lab. If Gary Jackson was right and Corey had been involved, they would find something.

* * *

The lab results from the clothing came back later in the week; Graham looked at the unopened envelope sitting on his desk as Holland handed him a coffee. He took a mouthful, laid the mug down, and exhaled. Gripping the envelope in his right hand, he ripped it open with great anticipation and studied the results.

"Shit, fuck and piss," the senior detective yelled.

"Nothing, Guv?" Holland didn't need to ask.

"Sweet fucking Fanny Adams. Not a trace of residue anywhere. He's fucking binned the clothes he was wearing, hasn't he?"

Holland wanted to tell his colleague he would probably have burned them. He wanted to say that he had suspected from the outset that Corey had been too calm and collected. But it wasn't his place to offer a comment. Graham was adamant that he had his man, and who was Holland to question his methods? It was back to the drawing board.

"Where do we go from here, Guv?" Holland asked.

Graham massaged his temples with his thumb and forefinger, leaned forward, and took another mouthful of coffee. He stood up and looked at his watch.

"Fancy a quick beer when we clock off?"

"Sure, Guv', why not?"

The Friday evening buzz filled London. They travelled on the tube to the Coach and Horses on Greek Street, Soho; one of their favourites, if not a little expensive. The atmosphere was spot on and a million miles from the job. It was the drinking den of the late Jeffrey Bernard, the *Spectator* columnist and the perfect place for a little thinking time. The pub was full.

They shouldn't have been talking shop, but it was all they had in common. Something convinced Graham they had missed a clue, but he didn't know what or where. Holland wasn't so sure.

"The only thing we have is the footage from the shop, and that's not the greatest quality in the world."

"It's not so bad, really. I can almost see the shape of Corey on there. We see him walk in and walk out. The shooter walks identical to Corey, even has the same build, but there isn't a criminal in history ever been convicted on the way he walks."

"I could look at it again, Guv', perhaps we've missed something."

Graham wouldn't have it. He said he'd studied the footage for hours.

"They're masked and wearing hoodies, for fuck's sake. Even if we could utilise facial recognition, it wouldn't be of any use."

They had next to nothing from the CCTV footage. Facial and iris recognition were not only controversial, but the European Court had also declared them infringements on human rights. What's more, the new technology that the Met had deployed was woefully inaccurate. A recent study had shown an eighty-one percent failure rate in some cases.

"And they were clever with their clothing too," Holland added.

"Yep, the clever cunts dressed head to toe in black, even their fucking shoes were black."

Holland thought for a moment. He was deep in thought and. Graham sensed it.

"What is it?"

Something had triggered a light bulb deep in Holland's subconscious as he mentally played back the grainy images on the CCTV footage from the jeweller's shop.

"What is it, man? Speak up." Graham jostled him.

Holland turned to him. His face was expressionless. "It's the CCTV, sir. We need to look at it again."

3

ABSENT FATHER

I had put six-year-old Oscar to bed. It was almost eight in the evening when a text came through from Shirley, a friend of Lee's sister.

She was in the area and wanted to see me immediately; she could be at my house in ten minutes.

I text her back. Sure, what's the problem?

Her one-word reply was, Lee

What the hell has he done now? I wondered.

My son's father, Lee, was about as unreliable as a father could be. We had separated four years before, and I was putting together a timetable of visits for him and Oscar to take place at a contact centre. I had taken him to court for maintenance. He had been playing hardball for years.

I opened the door to Shirley fifteen minutes later. She walked through to the kitchen, barely acknowledging my existence, and sat down at the table.

"What's he done this time?" I asked.

She looked up. "Got nicked."

I let out a sigh. "Not again. Tell me something that's gonna surprise me."

"This is bad," Shirley said. "Real bad."

I noticed a slight tremor flowing through my body. My knees weakened. I lowered myself onto the chair opposite her and picked up my half cup of semi-cold coffee.

"How bad?" I asked.

"You got anything to drink?" Shirley asked.

I pushed my chair back and rescued a bottle of white from the fridge as I pointed at the cupboard with the wine glasses.

"Tell me now, Shirley. I've just put Oscar to bed, and it's been a long day."

Lee had been involved in crime his entire life, but was one of London's clever criminals. He had a record, of course, spent some months inside, but nothing too heavy. He was a wheeler-dealer, sold drugs, handled stolen property, that sort of thing; at least that's what I had been led to believe. Nothing could have prepared me for what Shirley said next.

"Armed robbery," she announced. "They've nicked him for that job on New Bond Street a few months back."

He was out of my life, so why was I feeling so sick to the pit of my stomach?

Part of me wanted to say, *Good, it serves him right. He's bitten off more than he can chew this time.*

I had tried to tell him for years that he should put his intelligence to use in a straight business. I plonked the bottle on the kitchen table and, still holding the corkscrew, sank into my seat.

"No, not Lee," I whispered. "They've got the wrong guy."

Shirley sat down opposite, still holding the two glasses. "They don't think so. He's been picked out at an ID parade or something. CCTV, some shit like that."

"He's not capable."

And I believed every word that tumbled out of my mouth. The man was a liability, a risk-taker, but surely not an armed robber.

"What do you care anyway?" Shirley's words brought me back to the present. "He's out of your life for good now. Looks like the little fella won't be seeing his dad for a long time."

I told myself Shirley was right; I shouldn't care. Perhaps it was meant to be. With all the difficulties I'd been having with Lee lately, this was almost like a blessing. I was in a serious relationship; married to Pablo and now coping with a six-year-old and a baby. I didn't need his grief in my life.

By the time we drained the bottle, a couple of hours had passed. We had talked about the good and bad old days. I made it to bed, unsteady on my feet. Despite the alcohol, sleep wouldn't come.

4

THE CREATURE KNOWN AS MAN

I first met Harry when I was fourteen and on a school trip to the Italian Alps. It was the first time most of us had been away without our parents, so we revelled in the freedom. Our hotel had a disco on the ground floor and we could go until the ten o'clock curfew. Among the group partying were two tall, handsome Austrian guys. Harry was twenty, and his older brother, Max, was twenty-three. In the days after we met, they asked my classmate, Moira, and me to come to their flat and listen to Bob Marley's songs. Although I loved the idea, I was unsure of how I could leave when I wanted out. I refused to begin with. Moira was not so shy; she jumped at the chance.

One night around midnight, she strolled in, hair wet from having taken a shower. She disclosed she had lost her virginity that night to Max, just as I had feared might happen. They had listened to music, drunk copious amounts of wine and ended up in bed together.

I wasn't ready to be as adventurous with Harry, although he was the first boy I ever kissed properly. We got on well and started a long-distance relationship. By the time I was fifteen and still at boarding school; he was twenty-one and constantly on tour with his up-and-coming band. Harry had the potential to be an excellent musician and people were saying the band were going places. They played mostly at home but occasionally would perform around Europe.

We were wrapped up in each other, but I was still a virgin and, although in love; I wasn't quite ready to commit to him in the bedroom. He said he understood, after I explained my reluctance about us sleeping together. I went one step further. I told him I had no issues if he wanted to sleep with another girl (not too many times, I hoped) as long as he told me when it happened. Honesty and integrity were important to me; always had been.

He came back from a tour where the group had been performing with Boney M and Harry disclosed he had slept with one of the backing singers. I admired his honesty and said it was okay; and it was. I wanted a boyfriend I could trust and a man who would be straight with me; someone who was true to his word and on whom I could rely.

It wasn't easy dating a rock star. Every time I was in his company, there was someone else tagging along, someone else he couldn't seem to tear himself away from, someone else who he lavished attention on. She was always there, like a real person. I could never understand why a guitar had to be sexed, why it was female.

"It just is," he explained. "Guitars are female, BB King called his guitar Lucille. It's a fact."

He took that bloody guitar everywhere with him, and I mean everywhere. I once caught him playing it on the toilet. He was obsessed; that was a word I used often.

Harry was a gentleman at heart; he was okay to go at my pace and never pushed me into anything. I told him that when I lost my virginity; it was to be special. I didn't want to be like Moira, who got drunk at the party and gave herself away to a virtual stranger.

The band toured more often and sometimes the only contact we had was by letter; there was no social media in the 1980s. The demands on his time were escalating. He told his manager he had a relationship that was important to him and made sure he was home at my half-term break. Give him his due. He made a point of spending as much time as possible with me and when I could, I would try my best to get to UK gigs based in the South of England.

It was a classic rock and roll relationship and most of our dates were at gigs or the recording studio. And that bloody guitar was always there wherever we went; he even brought it to the pub with him and sat it on its own seat. I swear it was like another woman.

And the groupies; one around every corner, in every pub and every club.

"It's part of the scene," he said. "It's good for the image of the band."

One evening, we were together in Putney where some bloke was itching for a fight. He'd been shouting his mouth off about the 'waste of a space' black youths were in the area and I put him in his place with a well-timed comment that made him look small. It was a few days after the Brixton riots and tensions were running high.

He turned to Harry and said, "Your girlfriend is one rude bitch."

Before he had a chance to reply, the guy was on his feet and launched a blow or two towards poor Harry's face. Big mistake. It was a kind of slow-motion attack and Harry was not having any of it as he deflected the blows then punched him hard in the face. I jumped on the guy's back and beat him around the head as I kneed him continuously in the ribs. Within a minute or two, he'd fallen to the floor fighting for his breath, totally unprepared for the double onslaught, especially the one from behind. I was not the type of girl to stand by and watch some wanker hit my fella. That's what Harry was; my man.

It was over quickly, big mouth lying in a bloody, dazed heap on the floor. Two bouncers had intervened and pulled me off him; Harry had stepped back the minute the man hit the floor. Not me. I needed to make sure he didn't get back up. That was when a beaten man was at his most lethal.

Although the bouncers took our side when more than one patron explained that the man had attacked first, we were unceremoniously ushered out of the pub. We walked away holding hands, Harry was smiling but also a little shocked at seeing another side of his schoolgirl girlfriend.

"You can handle yourself," he said.

I nodded.

"Where did you learn to fight like that?"

I told him I didn't have a clue, although I could have confessed to having been the protector of my younger brother while we were at boarding school. I wouldn't allow anyone to hurt him, and the entire school knew it. It was in me. It was as simple as that. I'd fight to the death for anyone close to me, anyone I loved.

There was something about that night that was special and I wanted to show Harry how much he meant to me in every way. He had been patient and kind and had stuck to the rules. I loved him for that, and I needed to let him know how I felt. When we got back to my house, my dad was out. We kissed and cuddled as usual on the settee and I whispered in his ear, "Let's go upstairs."

I had never said that before and Harry knew what it meant; it just felt right and I was over the legal age limit by then. What else was I waiting for? Who else would I risk my life for if not for him? Harry asked me if I was sure; I smiled and nodded.

He carried me upstairs and laid me on the bed. I felt safe with him, albeit a little nervous. There was nothing else I wanted to do at that moment than to give myself to him. I pulled off my top and undid his belt. He kissed me passionately, and we continued to take off each other's clothes, kissing with every garment that was thrown onto the floor. As he penetrated me, searing pain shot through me, which gave way, not to pleasure but to something that was at least a little more bearable. It hadn't looked like that in films but, after a while, there was no pain, which was a relief. To be honest, the first time was not what I had expected it to be. But every time after that, it was pure pleasure, and I loved it.

Soon after, he wrote a song for me, 'Girl'. He sang it, even though he was the lead guitarist. It was on the B side of their first single. I was thrilled to bits.

As time went on, I had a nagging thought that he was being unfaithful and not keeping up his end of the bargain by telling me things. That trust and honesty we once had seemed to evaporate. He was away for longer periods and there were times he didn't make contact for weeks.

When he did come back home, I noticed his eyes had started to wander and there always seemed to be a pretty girl or two hanging around the band. I wanted more. Loyalty and honesty were important to me, and I wondered if it was time to finish our relationship.

At yet another after party, I had seen enough. He was flirting with other girls, hardly paying me any attention. We had a big row, and I told him it was over. He didn't believe me. He didn't know me that well and I walked out of the party and his life forever.

Our relationship had lasted three years. It was fun, but it was always going to end badly because of the environment we were part of. Even though it broke my heart, I stood by my decision and principles. This wasn't the life I wanted; it was time to move on. I wanted to have fun, so I dated a few guys, but there was no one special.

* * *

At eighteen, I left home and rented a flat in Tooting. I joined an Insurance Broker in Streatham and became one of their top salespeople. When I was nineteen, I got a mortgage through them to buy my own two-bedroom flat a short walk from the office. Life was good. I was prospecting for clients in Clapham, knocking on doors. It was a numbers game. If you knocked on enough doors, you were bound to make a sale. My smart appearance and charm always got me in the door, and the day I met David was no exception.

I did my pitch after he invited me in. He took the bait and said he wanted a policy and, as he signed on the dotted line, he invited me out that weekend. He said he was in-between jobs, and I accepted that. I never actually asked what he did. It didn't matter, he was too good-looking to pass by.

He picked me up from my flat in his blue BMW on the Saturday. He was wearing Farah trousers, black patent leather shoes, the silk socks that the cool guys liked to wear, and a black shirt with some sort of pattern in it. I wore a purple elasticated dress with thin diamond-jewelled straps; it hugged every curve on my body. I wore silver shoes with kitten heels and carried a small diamond-speckled clutch bag. We went to a club where they played my kind of music to about 200 people.

David was mixed-raced and drop-dead gorgeous. He was the man of my dreams. Tall, with thick, dark, curly hair, long eyelashes, and a small beard. At twenty-four, he had the most amazing green eyes which ran in his family. He was educated and sophisticated, one of six children, mostly girls, and his parents were from Jamaica and Ireland.

Wouldn't you know it, David was a good dancer too and he smelled amazing as we danced in sync to the rhythm of the music. It was a warm summer's night and we hit it off straight away. It was so perfect. David took charge and I liked that. I am quite an independent person and like to have my own way but what I wanted was a man to take charge of me, to challenge me and David was that man.

We were soon seeing each other more often. He would come over to my flat in the evening and stay until the morning. He was still in-between jobs and I would often leave him in bed while I went to my day's appointments. We met each other's family and friends; we were definitely an item. His mum was a lovely lady and treated me like her own.

One day, he announced that he was a Muslim and told me all about the teachings of Islam. I was fascinated and sometimes we would talk about his faith well into the small hours of the morning.

Then things turned bleak, slowly at first. I saw my friends less; then they stopped calling me altogether. This was perhaps because David would start an argument with them, particularly Camilla, who was a born-again Christian. Camilla was a colleague, and she had been trying for a while to get me to come to her church. She and David would get into heated arguments about religion. It was ridiculous.

Eventually, I noticed we weren't going out anymore, we stayed at his house. David had a lot of time on his hands and would spend it with his friends, doing what I didn't know.

One morning, as I was getting ready to go to work, David asked me not to go. I said I couldn't do that; I had a mortgage to pay and needed to work. But he turned angry and was saying irrational things to me; accusing me of having an affair with the men at work and wanting to attract every man on the street by the clothes I was wearing. He lashed out at me after I told him he was an idiot.

At first, I was stunned.

This wasn't the first time a man had hit me. Philip,

a manager at work who had taken a liking to me, had hit me once before. He was handsome and drove a gold Ford Capri, from which he would boom out the Nina Simone song: 'My baby just cares for me!' To a young girl, he was edgy and exciting in his three-piece suit. He impressed me. I was in his team, along with Camilla. She was dating someone else from another branch in Camberwell. Philip and I started seeing each other after our team's visit to Paris, a weekend trip for all the top earners in the company, in recognition of their hard work. After that, we saw each other regularly.

Initially, Philip was in a relationship and they had a child together, but he moved out, back to his parent's house, and so we were an item. He'd mention marriage and suggested we get engaged, although there was no ring yet. I think he said that to convince me to stay with him, but then one evening when he had had too much to drink, we got into an argument and he hit me in the face and gave me a black eye. That relationship ended immediately.

But this was different. I loved David and I couldn't understand why he was saying such things. So, I counted to ten and composed myself, trying to take in exactly what had happened. But I couldn't contain myself; I hit back, punching him in the nose, following up with a slap, breaking my nails. He had a large scratch down the side of his neck. He came for me again and I fought him off. We struggled and fought and I screamed at him, telling him how ridiculous his allegations sounded.

'How can you throw these accusations at me? I'm with you practically twenty-four-seven. I don't go anywhere without you, so you know what I'm doing all the time!' I yelled at him.

Eventually, it all calmed down and he apologised profusely, saying he didn't know what had come over him and that he would never do that again. I believed him and he persuaded me to call in sick. We stayed in bed, making mad, passionate, crazy love for the rest of the day.

Soon after that incident, he asked me to marry him. His proposal shocked me and I didn't see it coming. I loved him, but at twenty, I told him I was too young to get married. We talked about it, then he changed the subject.

5

A CHANGE OF FAITH

However, things between us were not completely resolved.

The accusations of me wanting other guys, of dressing to attract men, or wearing make-up increased with the arguments; I only wore a little eyeliner and mascara.

How on earth can I prove I love him? I thought to myself.

The situation was affecting my job, and I had no one to turn to. I couldn't concentrate. I tensed during the mornings because David insisted on meeting me every day for lunch. He would wait across the road from my office and if a man came in or out the door at the same time as me he would start an argument over our meal, calling me disgusting and saying I wanted to get into bed with all the men around me.

I felt I had to prove that he had it all wrong, that I wasn't interested in other men. I loved him despite all the arguments, would do anything to please him. So, I did the ultimate. I joined him and became a Muslim.

In the Muslim faith, women are actively discouraged from wearing makeup and their hair has to be covered in public. It wasn't too difficult because, for me, there was no one but David. I was not the type to have affairs. I was faithful, and I wanted to prove my loyalty to him. In one month, I read the Koran from cover to cover and learned, among other philosophies, why clothing could attract unwanted attention from men. I stopped wearing tight-fitting tops and such like, but had to look smart for my job.

One day, after I had stayed over with him and as I was getting ready for work, another argument started and he went into a rage. I left and as I passed the basement window to climb the steps to the street, he punched through the glass from inside. Everything seemed to happen in slow motion; shards of glass hung in the air as they flew towards me. I waited for the pain, the blood; his fist stopped inches from my face. Miraculously, not one piece of glass touched me. I was petrified and ran as fast as my legs would carry me. He had taken things to another level. I had to get away from this man. I was convinced that one day he would kill me if I stayed around.

I couldn't go to work that day; I needed to escape

to a sanctuary and get my head straight. The phone rang when I opened the door after returning to my flat. I didn't answer. A while later, David came over and buzzed the intercom, but I refused to answer it; I felt safe because my flat was on the second floor. He banged on the door of the main building; no one answered. Then he came round the back and I heard his footsteps coming up the fire escape.

I was petrified and reached for the phone to dial 999 but it was dead. I later found out that he'd cut the phone wire. I rushed out the front door to the neighbour's flat, banging on their door and begging them to call for help; I stayed with them until the police arrived. The two officers were understanding; they searched the perimeter of the building but David had long gone. They started talking about arrests and convictions, but I didn't want to press charges. I had calmed down and said I'd overreacted and that it had been a lover's tiff. I told them about my phone being dead and they found where the phone wire had been cut outside and fixed it. Then they left.

A few days later, David and I made up. He said he was sorry, that he loved me and that it wouldn't happen again; I believed him. Every fibre in my body wanted to trust him and things were okay for a while.

I had lost my job by this time because I was not committed and was no longer giving my best.

Then one night, he arrived at my house in a rage again. I had no idea why until he said that I fancied his sister's boyfriend. Yet another ridiculous accusation. As the row escalated, I shouted and screamed at him. I had had enough. I told him it was over this time and that I never wanted to see him again.

We were standing in my kitchen by the drainer, which was full of cutlery. He turned to the left and picked up a large carving knife, saying no one else could have me if he couldn't. He told me he would kill me or put me in a wheelchair. I pleaded with him to be reasonable and begged for my life. I tried to explain to him that the countless accusations were without logic. I was a Muslim and went to the mosque with him every Friday, even learning Arabic and I had committed myself to the faith. All because I loved *him*. But he wasn't listening to any of it. He hadn't worked a day since I first met him and was smoking weed a lot. As he stood a few feet from me holding the knife to my face, it petrified me and I wondered how I had got into this situation.

At first, he had been the man I had dreamed of but, over time, he had turned into a monster who had driven my friends away and threatened to burn my dad's house down if I ever told him what had happened between us. I was trapped by this maniac and I had nowhere to go.

After much talking and pleading, I managed to get into my bedroom and crawled under the duvet. He stood at the end of my bed with the 10-inch kitchen knife in his hand, looking at me with cold eyes. I drifted off to sleep eventually, wondering if I'd ever see the light of day again.

When I woke up, he was sitting on the floor by the bedroom door. The knife lay on the carpet beside him. When he saw I was awake, he didn't say anything, but he got to his feet and left. Confused and in shock, I knew I had to get away from this man. But how?

By this stage, it was impossible to share my desperate state with friends and family; I had no one I could confide in. David had seen to that saying if I told my family, they would be next, or so I thought. With my confidence at rock bottom, I didn't have the resolve to see past the day that lay ahead. I had no fight left in me. He threatened to kill me every time he showed up. I was so depressed that I had stopped eating and made an appointment with my GP to ask for help; he threatened to send me to hospital if I didn't start eating and putting on weight. I couldn't tell him the real reason.

In a moment of clarity, I went to Maudsley Mental Health Hospital to seek refuge and begged them to take me in. All I wanted was to feel safe. The doctors listened to why I wanted to admit myself, but they concluded that I was not crazy, just sad and frightened. They refused my request.

Lost and in a dark place, I was in fear of my life. I succumbed to the notion that I was going to die and decided that if that was my fate, then I would rather do it myself than let that crazy man take my life. I stopped at the chemist and bought a twenty-four packet of Anadin, went back to my flat, made a cup of tea, and swallowed the lot.

A few minutes after I had taken them, they started to affect me. A feeling of tiredness washed over me and I felt drained. I staggered through to the lounge and collapsed onto the settee; I wanted to sleep and never wake up.

But, I woke up with the sun streaming through my lounge window. Surprisingly, I felt fine, but I was angry that I hadn't died. I so much wanted the nightmare to end.

Common sense kicked in and I thought I should phone for an ambulance, convinced that my organs would begin to shut down and that I'd end up in agony while fully conscious. I dialled 999 and told the operator what I had done. She sent an ambulance immediately, and I walked out to it, protesting that there was nothing wrong with me.

I was taken to the local hospital but still felt okay as I was wheeled into A&E. They told me I needed my stomach pumped. The staff described how they'd have to put a tube down my throat; the thought of that made me feel terrible, and I wanted to be sick. I rushed into the toilet, deposited a load of brown vomit into the pan and, I suspect, most of the tablets. They put me into bed for observations. I felt so alone, but the place was clean and I felt so safe there that I dozed off for a while.

A commotion outside my room wakened me; David was trying to get in. He pushed two nurses out of the way and made it to the door. "I'm fucking going to kill you," he screamed at me.

I was terrified. Why hadn't the tablets worked? Why was this still happening to me? A couple of security guards wrestled him away from the area and threw him out. I later found out that one of his mother's friends worked at the hospital and had seen me; she told his mum.

My dad didn't know what had happened; I didn't want him to know about David. I wanted to protect my dad and his house from going up in flames. Only my aunt knew and, despite begging her not to tell my dad, she did and he came to collect me from the hospital. Although I didn't want to talk, I eventually blurted out the full story and why I had ended up doing what I did.

Dad took me to my aunt's house in Balham because David didn't know about her or where she lived. My aunt and dad knew my life was in danger so, between them, they devised another plan that I would go and stay with other family members in Sweden.

When the time came, my dad drove me to Gatwick Airport. I still don't know how David found out, but as I was at airport security saying a tearful goodbye to my dad, he appeared, shouting at the top of his voice. This time he was begging me not to go and threatening to kill himself if I did. Dad shoved me towards the security gate where he knew David couldn't get through. I breathed again when I saw the airport's armed police and knew that peace was at the end of a plane trip.

And yet, as the plane took to the air, I felt conflicted because, as much as I was in fear of this man, I didn't want him to kill himself because of me. If I could have asked the pilot to turn back to London I would have done so several times during that flight although I was more than aware I needed to save myself first.

As we approached Stockholm, I looked out of the small window at the snowy landscape below me; I had done the right thing. But why did it hurt so much? How had all that happened and how did my dream man turn into such a monster? I vowed that day I would never let a man dominate and control me again. I would get a gun and shoot any man who dared to try.

I stayed in Sweden for some months and, when I eventually returned to the UK, I enrolled in a college in West London and met the girls with whom I would continue to have friendships for a long time. We partied every weekend, but a male relationship was the furthest thing from my mind. It was nice having girlfriends again. At weekends, we raved like there was no tomorrow from midnight until six in the morning. We followed the sound system Rappatack. Our fun didn't involve men; we had zero interest in them and thankfully, David faded into the deepest recesses of my mind.

However, there was no shortage of male attention.

Without sounding biased, I knew I had the look that men liked. Ever since I was a little girl, my mum had told me I was the perfect blend, a mixed-race creation of African-Caribbean and Scandinavian thanks to my parents meeting on the banks of the River Thames in Kingston at a dance one starry night! Several model agencies had already shown an interest in me. My portfolio read I had a 'striking lithe figure with eyes that are a deep earthy brown and burn with an internal flame.' Their words not mine.

I had long, thick, curly black hair, the sort that formed perfect corkscrew ringlets every time it got wet. When the sun shone on my hair, it had gold and copper undertones and radiated light. My gran once told me that women would die for hair like mine. I didn't understand what she meant at the time. To me, it was thick and unmanageable. But I liked the uniqueness of it, and random strangers would often compliment me. My hair drew attention, and I liked that. As I grew older, I realised what my gran meant.

The offers of dates came flooding in, but I was too raw from the breakup with David. I had a lot of male friends, really nice guys, but I made it clear I just wanted a brother and sister type relationship, just good friends. My attitude offended some of them; they didn't understand and never came near me again.

But, I still enjoyed male company, always had. Men were less prone to being 'bitches' because, for some unknown reason, females carry more of the jealous genes than their male counterparts.

I was heading to a Children in Need concert with two of my best friends when I bumped into someone who would change every aspect of my future. To say he would shape the rest of my life would be a complete understatement.

"Where the hell are those two?" I muttered to myself as I sat in the car with the engine running.

I looked at my watch again. "Always late, always bloody late."

I looked in my rear-view mirror and noticed a car coming towards me. It slowed down and pulled up alongside me; the passenger wound down his window. My heart skipped a beat. *Cute*, I thought.

The man was dark and handsome, looked a bit like Eddie Murphy and I couldn't help but smile.

I wound my window down. "What is it?" I asked.

He flashed a smile of perfectly white, straight Hollywood teeth. "Where you heading tonight?"

"A concert with my friends. We're going to see Aswad," I said confidently, showing off a bit.

The tickets were like gold dust.

"So, a date is out of the question?"

"You got that right."

"What about Friday?" he persevered. "Would you like to go to a Freaky Party with me? It will be a whole lot more fun than an Aswad Concert."

I didn't have a clue what a Freaky Party was, but I wasn't about to let 'cutey' see that.

"And what makes you think I want to go to a Freaky Party with you?"

He smiled again. As our eyes met, I felt a tingle run the length of my spine. I smiled back. I couldn't help myself.

Shit, I thought.

"This your house?"

I nearly said it's just a bedsit but bit my tongue. "Yes."

"I'll pick you up at seven then."

I nodded. "Okay."

The car sped off.

Why did I just say that? I scolded myself.

I didn't even know the guy; he could have been a mass murderer and now he knew exactly where I lived.

"What's a Freaky Party?" I asked my friends when they eventually turned up ten minutes late.

They didn't have a clue either. I told them all about the Eddie Murphy lookalike and we headed off to the concert. Aswad played an impressive set. They were on stage for nearly two hours. I couldn't recall a single song they had played when folk asked about the gig the following day. I only had one thing on my mind; my date. I tried to play it cool but had to admit to myself I was excited as hell. What was it with this man? I had talked to him for less than a minute.

I was ready way before seven. At ten past, I was getting a little annoyed, but by half-past, I was absolutely fuming. I had never been stood up before.

How dare he, I thought.

At eight o'clock I wondered if I had perhaps heard

the wrong time and waited until eight-thirty.

At nine o'clock, I headed for town with my two best friends and I consigned Eddie Murphy to history. He was just another guy, I told myself. Nothing a few hours on the dance floor wouldn't put right. I knew the right sound systems and the best places, so we danced all night long. Eventually, we called it a day as the sun came up and made our way home.

It was some weeks later when my landlady stopped me in the street and said that someone had called on me. I was annoyed. I had a strict rule in force. Nobody called at my house unless they were invited. I was even more annoyed when the landlady explained it had been a man.

"A tall, black fellow," she explained.

I had two 'tall, black friends' and stormed down to the payphone at the bottom of the street to call them both. It wasn't them, they said, and I believed them. I wondered. Was Eddie Murphy back on the scene? He was. I was out when he called again a few days later. He had told my landlady we had a mutual friend, Steve, who lived at the bottom of the road and that he would be there most of the day. My curiosity got the better of me and later that evening, I walked down to Steve's. My dream man opened the door.

"Hi, I'm Lee," he said. "And what's your name?"

I told him my name was Caroline, then added, "But my friends call me Cookie."

"I can see why." He smiled.

6

THE ENIGMA

I had heard of love at first sight, but always had my doubts. It was the stuff of movies, Pretty Woman, Bridget Jones' Diary, that sort of thing. But now, I guess at twenty-two; I wasn't so sure. It started slowly at first. We met at Steve's house now and again and just talked, but something was happening to the chemicals in my body each time I set eyes on him or he came within a few feet of me. My body flooded with feel-good hormones, dopamine, serotonin and oxytocin even when we only played blackjack, which I would often win. What the hell was going on?

But I fought against my instincts. I would never give in easily. I was still annoyed at being stood up, and without explanation, on what should have been our first date. I played it cool, and told him I wasn't interested, but inside my heart was turning summersaults; there was an electric, almost animalistic, attraction towards him.

I noticed his intelligence immediately. He differed from the other guys I had dated and, from the outset, our conversations almost turned into an academic competition of the minds. It was point scoring on a basic level. We tried to outwit or outsmart each other and I almost felt like throwing in the towel and telling him he'd won. But that would never happen. We were as stubborn as each other.

It was as if Lee had filled an intellectual void. There was a definite stimulus taking place each time I sat down with him. No man I had ever dated made me feel like that. He was charming and confident and above all; he made me laugh. He was strong, fit and ingenious and, of course, incredibly handsome. If my friends ever asked what the best bit about him was, that was easy.

"His arse!" I replied.

Without a doubt, he had the sexiest arse on the planet.

But he had a dark side that I knew nothing about. I had never asked about his job or his profession. I had touched on the subject once or twice but never got a specific answer other than he was a businessman.

"What business?" I had asked.

He shrugged his shoulders and grinned. "This and that, Cookie. I have a few business interests. I'm in partnership with a couple of guys."

"What sort of partnership?"

"Sales mostly, we buy and sell."

"Sell what? Cars, property?"

He side tracked me.

In the meantime, Homer, my good friend, warned me off. He had called me and suggested a drink in one of the local wine bars. He'd heard just how far the relationship with Lee was going. Friends had told him I was wrapped up in Lee. They had said that I was in love.

I knew as soon as I saw his face that something was bothering him. He ordered a couple of drinks and we sat down at a table in the corner of the bar, far away from twitching ears or prying eyes.

"It's Lee," he started. "He's bad news."

Nothing like beating about the bush, I thought.

"So tell me," I prompted him.

He hadn't gone into detail about why Lee was bad news or what exactly he was involved in. I defended him.

"He's a businessman, Homer. He's a bit over-confident and cocky, but he acts and dresses like a businessman. Anyone can see that. Okay, so some of his business deals may be dodgy, but aren't all businessmen a little bent?"

Homer took a drink and laughed. "Not as bent as Lee."

"What do you mean by that?" I bit back.

But the conversation didn't progress beyond that initial stage. Homer had said Lee was a bit of an enigma and not the sort of person I'd want to cross. We didn't exactly fall out, but there was a distinct frostiness as we said goodbye. Homer said he didn't want to interfere; he was only looking out for me because he cared so much and didn't want to see me get hurt.

I kissed him on the cheek. "Catch up soon."

Homer nodded. I turned and walked away.

"Be careful," he shouted after me. "You can do better than that."

Homer had annoyed me. Was he jealous? I had long suspected that he had a soft spot for me. Was it just a little envy creeping in? I would make a point of asking Lee all about his business interests. After all, we were more or less an item now. Surely I had a right to know.

I was falling deeply in love with Lee. I loved everything about him. His skin was dark like ebony and silky smooth like chocolate, exactly like a Bournville Chocolate bar and, at work, I often used to daydream about what had happened the night before. At lunchtime, I'd buy a bar of Bournville Chocolate for no other reason than it reminded me of him.

Within weeks, he was my bed-mate, but I thought it was strange that he had nowhere to stay. He told me he had fallen out with his landlord and 'in between' properties. He stayed with a mate for the interim period, but more often than not persuaded me to let him stay at mine. I wasn't complaining and, to be honest, I couldn't get enough of him. He was tall and strong with rippling muscles, and the more I got, the more I wanted. The sex was electrifying. I had heard the expression that the earth moved, but I thought it was just that, an expression, but with Lee, I really felt it. It was more than the earth moving. When we made love, it was like being out in space in some other part of the universe in another stratosphere.

By now we were seeing each other every night. When I quizzed him about his work, everything seemed to be kosher and legitimate.

Each morning he would shower and change, normally into an expensive suit. He would plan his working day in a diary, booking appointments with other businessmen or map out journeys to places like Watford or Peterborough. He left for work at the same time as me or earlier. Sometimes he would drive me to work. At nights, he'd come home and tell me about deals and business he had attended to, although he never went into specific details.

We had become wrapped up in each other. I was addicted to him and I couldn't get enough and although he played it cool with me sometimes, he was just as hooked. On Valentine's Day, he brought me some flowers and a mug. It read:

Exceptional Woman

I was, and he knew it, as did all his friends. There was no one like me. Ever since I was a small child, I knew I was different from anyone else and when it came to love and best friends and family you got one hundred and ten percent from me... pure devotion. I was committed all the way and for Lee it was great news because all I wanted was to be with him.

I was prepared to do anything to be with Lee so, when he introduced me to drugs, I didn't object. Once or twice previously, he had offered me weed. I had tried a little coke but I wasn't that into it. Weed and hash were fine, especially at night after a particularly stressful day at work, but the coke wasn't for me. He insisted; he persuaded me to take some before we went to bed early one night. It would make the sex better.

He wasn't wrong. It was as if every nerve was on fire, tingling; oh my God, what was happening to me? Having sex while high was on a different level and I liked it; I liked it a lot. Too much actually, and that bothered me, not being in control of myself, so I didn't take it again. I always had to be in control of my faculties.

Life was sweet. I couldn't have been happier. I'd work, think about him, go to the gym, eat and then we'd meet up at my place or his mate's house. By now his mates were my mates too. I got on well with every one of them; they respected me. They found themselves in awkward situations at times, their loyalty was divided. When I wanted to know where Lee was because he was late or hadn't shown up, I would demand that they tell me. Some of them had misgivings about dropping him in it.

In time, they grew to realise I didn't take any shit,

and they'd give me a story about where he was. Lee was my man. It was as simple as that. If he failed to show up on a date, I'd find out where he was. Normally, he was having an extra beer with the lads, but that didn't matter to me. I would go to wherever he was and cause a ruckus. Men didn't intimidate me. I could physically stand up to them and sometimes I did just that.

On one occasion when he was more than an hour late, I found out he was at a house party, jumped in my car and gate crashed it. Lee was laughing and having a good time with his mates and appeared oblivious as I sat down on the opposite side of the room. Memories of being stood up by him when we first met came flooding back and this time he felt my wrath.

I waited, two minutes, three minutes. I waited a full five minutes before I snapped. I screamed and lunged at him yelling at the top of my voice calling him all the names under the sun, punching him as hard as I could wherever I could get bodily contact. He was a seasoned fighter and I don't think my punches had much effect on him but he didn't show it. The colour drained from his face as he grabbed both my arms, begging me to stay cool. He lifted me and took me outside and forced me into his car to calm down. I was fuming; I didn't want to calm down and insisted he let me out.

He locked the doors and point-blank refused. He must have thought I would calm down in a few minutes. He didn't know me that well because I refused to speak to him. It was a battle of wits and stubbornness. He kept me in the car for hours, refusing to let me leave. I told him it was over; a well-used line of mine.

"I never fucking want to see you again!" I shouted over and over again.

He knew it wasn't over. He knew how much I loved him.

It got later. He kept telling me he had forgotten the time and that nothing happened at the party, but I stood my ground and told him if he said he was meeting me at a certain time, I would expect nothing less.

As the sun rose at the bottom of the street and the early morning rays flooded into the car, he released the central locking system and I climbed out. I slammed the door and once again yelled that I never wanted to see him again.

But I did. These were hollow words said without an ounce of conviction. He was too sweet and cute to give up so easily and I loved him as I have loved no one before.

When we next met, I demanded to know what he was all about and insisted he tell me the truth. He had kept me completely in the dark. I knew nothing of his life.

Then the admission came. Lee's main retail product was drugs. He dealt in anything: weed, coke and even the harder stuff. It all turned a healthy profit and Lee knew exactly how to play the system to make sure he wasn't active on the streets doing the pushing. Lee supplied the suppliers; he was at the top of the tree and intended to stay there. He played the out-of-sight and out-of-mind game.

I found out he dealt in stolen goods too. In short, Lee's profession was that of a criminal. It was all he had ever known; he'd never worked an honest day in his life since he left school at sixteen.

7

THE BUSINESSMAN

Looking back at the incident in the car, I believe on my part it was pure rage; one borne out of the fact I loved him so much and didn't want to lose him. As I drove to that party, breaking every speed limit along the way, I imagined the unimaginable that he was with another girl. He wasn't, of course, he was with his mates, but my temper had built up so much that I erupted like a volcano.

A few days later, we were back together. I'd bumped into him in a local bar. We smiled and fell into each other's arms.

"I'm sorry," he said. "It was my fault."

"No, it was my fault."

"No, it wasn't. It was mine."

Within five minutes, and like teenagers, we were

out of the pub and heading back to my house for two or three hours of making up. We had had our fair share of breakups in the first couple of years of our relationship, but the making-up part was simply magical and everything that had gone before was simply forgotten. I sincerely believed that our love was stronger; nothing would ever break us apart.

Lee's business interests were taking up more and more of his time. Apart from dealing in drugs and a bit of stolen property, I still didn't know exactly what business he was in, but I was about to find out.

His friend Roger, was always around. They would disappear into the kitchen and have conversations that I couldn't hear, purposely keeping their voices down. I was becoming concerned. Roger would even turn up just before we were heading to bed and tell Lee that some urgent business had cropped up. Without any explanation, Lee would be off out the door and maybe wouldn't come back until four or five o'clock in the morning. He'd try to slip into bed quietly but I was always awake, I never slept a wink when he wasn't by my side. One week, he had three of these night-time business meetings and I was shattered. I decided to have it out with him over breakfast. As well as working all day every day, I was also modelling for a couple of magazines. On the Friday morning, Lee made some coffee and handed me a cup.

"We can't go on like this," I said. "You're gonna break me."

"What's up, babe?" he said innocently.

"What's up?" I shouted. "You know what's up. That's three nights this week where I haven't slept a wink. I feel like shit and I look like shit and my work is suffering too. I have a meeting with my boss; he wants to know what is going on."

He shrugged his shoulders and took a mouthful of coffee.

"I can't sleep because I don't know where you are or who you are with."

He put his cup on the table. "Okay, so if I tell you what I'm doing and where I am, will you be able to sleep?"

"It depends on what you are up to," I said.

I think at this point I sensed he was up to no good, but nothing could have prepared me for what he said next.

"We break into houses."

"What?"

"Roger and me. We burgle people's houses. That's what we do at nights."

My cup slipped from my grasp and dropped on the table. There was coffee everywhere and words failed me. He had said it so casually as if he had been shopping at a twenty-four-hour supermarket.

"We go for the rich set; it's more about the thrill than what we get."

I sat in stunned silence as he told me all about their burglary business. He told me the type of places they targeted and how good the buzz was, walking around people's houses as they slept. He told me how they only went for cash and jewellery, particularly expensive watches. They were the easiest to move on.

All I could think of was losing him if he got caught.

"But you'll go to jail, Lee, and I couldn't handle that."

"I won't get caught, never been caught yet," he said confidently.

I couldn't believe what I was hearing.

He had a towel in his hand and wiped up the coffee. After a few minutes, I found my voice. I wouldn't let him go now that I had him talking. And talk he did. He told me about his other business interests. He explained the burglary and fencing stolen goods as if he was telling me about working in a bank or an insurance broker. This was a nightmare. He told me how lucrative it all was, how he made thousands each week and no job that he was qualified to do would pay that sort of money. At least that bit was true because he wasn't qualified for anything; this had been his business since he left school.

I fought back tears. My illusion of a lifetime together was disappearing down the drain. I looked up. I was staring into the eyes of a hardened career criminal. It got worse.

Lee poured me another coffee and proceeded to tell me about his protection racket. He named the businesses in the local area and further afield, businesses where he took money for protection. He made it sound so noble, but I knew exactly what protection money was. If the businesses didn't pay their dues, they would be burgled or set on fire. Some protection rackets simply used the threat of physical violence on the owner. But Lee said he didn't. He tried to justify his business as he explained that if he didn't run the protection racket, someone else would simply step in.

"It's just business, it's expected, part of the outlay of running a business."

He talked me through the maths. He had more than twenty businesses paying him a regular monthly amount.

"I don't take the piss and I genuinely look after them. One of my shops was burgled last month and I found out who did it."

As proud as punch, Lee said he found the burglar, 'sorted him out' and took everything he'd stolen back to the shop.

"The shop owner was delighted; I promised him that the burglar would never come near him or his shop again."

More coffee, I needed more coffee, in fact I needed something stronger.

Our conversation lasted over two hours. Before I was due to leave for work, I phoned in sick. Lee grinned as he reminded me he didn't have a boss to answer to.

It's difficult to explain how I felt. It was as if I didn't know him anymore. I'd never probed deep into his business interests until that Friday. Perhaps I sensed there was something not quite right and didn't want to hear the truth. But now I had it. It was out in the open. I put my head in my hands and sobbed.

I painted pictures of him getting caught either burgling houses or being set up as he went to collect his protection money. The police made a big thing whenever they pulled off a sting to trap protection racketeers. The sentences were stiff, ten years plus, considered by the police to be one of the really low forms of criminality. I was aware of a tremble pulsing through my body. I closed my eyes as I pictured Lee in the dock, in the back of a prison van, in jail.

"I don't want you to go to jail. I couldn't live without you."

"I won't be going to jail, babe. I'm too clever. I've covered every base."

And that was what annoyed me. He *was* clever. He was clever and disciplined, had a good work ethic and put the hours in. He approached his criminal activities in the same way a successful business person would. He was no different.

I begged him to go straight. "You've been lucky; you've never been caught, so get out while you can. You've clearly got money behind you, so invest it into something straight."

I told him he would make a success of anything he tried. He told me it wasn't that easy.

"Why?" I asked

"I have a criminal record."

"You what? For fuck's sake, you said they had

never caught you."

"It was a long time ago. I'm smarter now."

"What happened?"

"I burgled a Post Office and they had CCTV."

"For fuck's sake...!"

He tried to calm me down as I paced around the kitchen like a caged animal. I didn't know what to say. I wanted to throw him out, but I loved him like crazy and couldn't imagine life without him.

It came to me after a few minutes. "If you burgled a Post Office you must have done jail time?

"Yes," he nodded, "just a couple of years."

Just a couple of years, I let the thought go around in my head.

He said it... as if he had been taking a fortnight's holiday in Tenerife.

I told him to leave and cried for the rest of the day. It wasn't the fact that I had discovered that the man I loved was a criminal. It was worse than that because now I felt I didn't know him. Everything I had perceived of him had been shattered in the space of a few hours. He had lied and deceived me. We spent a week apart.

He knocked on my door one afternoon; he smiled as he apologised. "I'm sorry, Cookie, I am what I am, but now you know the whole truth."

He told me he only kept it from me to protect me. My rage had dissipated over the week. I had calmed down. I invited him in and within half an hour we were in bed together, making up.

We ironed things out during the next few weeks. I told him I wanted nothing to do with his criminal activities, nor did I want to enjoy the benefits of his crimes. There were strict rules in place. I was working, earning decent money, and I needed nothing from him financially. To be honest, the drug dealing didn't affect me too badly. I told myself it wasn't any worse than burgling people's houses in the middle of the night or taking money from struggling businessmen and so, reluctantly, I accepted that my man was a criminal. I just prayed to God that he knew what he was doing and would never get caught. I couldn't bear the thought of him going to prison.

8

BLIND LOVE

Lee continued to burgle houses. Or at least I thought he did. Sometimes he arrived back home at three, four, five in the morning, but other times it was much later, early to mid-morning. When I questioned him, he would tell me he had been to houses further afield, that the early morning traffic had caused delays. I wasn't so sure. Burgling houses in the middle of the night was the perfect cover for a man cheating on his woman.

I began to get suspicious, possibly even paranoid. I knew just how attractive Lee was to other girls but when I quizzed him about his 'all-nighters' he would always deny that he was up to no good and swore blind that he would never betray me. He told me I was all he ever wanted. He told me the words my heart was crying out for. I convinced myself that he had the same morals as me and that he would never be unfaithful. Infidelity was crossed off my list of suspicions. We were made from the same mould; we were made for each other.

It started with a burning sensation when I went to the toilet. I thought nothing of it at first, perhaps something I ate or drank. The following morning, it was still there. In fact, it was ten times worse. My God, I had never experienced anything like it. I put it down to a urine infection and drank gallons of water in an attempt to flush it out of my system. The following day, I went to my doctor. She examined me and delivered the bad news.

"It's a sexually transmitted disease I'm afraid."

"Impossible," I reacted. "You must be wrong."

She shook her head. She'd probably been through the same scenario a hundred times. The poor, loyal, faithful wife or girlfriend, the shock on her face as the penny drops and she realises her man has been cheating.

"You're sure?"

"I'm one hundred percent sure, and unless you spend twenty-four hours a day with your boyfriend, I'm afraid it isn't so impossible."

She gave me a prescription, told me it should clear up in a few days. I was speechless. I couldn't believe it. I was numb with shock. How could he do this to me?

As Lee walked into the kitchen that evening, I

flung the first cup in his direction. He palmed it away; it smashed into the wall but that didn't stop me throwing another three. He yelped in pain as the last one bounced off his head.

"Babe, what is it? What's wrong?"

I pushed the prescription across the table and he looked down and it registered.

"You've given me a sexually transmitted disease, Lee. Thank you very much."

"But I... I—" he stuttered.

The man who was never short of words was lost because he knew me and how loyal and faithful I was. He knew I adored him, worshiped the very ground he walked on, and that I had never even looked at another man. I had everything I wanted in him.

I surprised myself. Suddenly I was calm. "Why, Lee?"

"I... she... she was—"

"She meant nothing to you. That's what you want to say, isn't it?"

"Yes... I—"

"The old line, eh? You made a dreadful mistake; it was a one-off and it's never going to happen again."

He nodded. His moist eyes looked doleful; he sat down and reached across the table for my hands. I pulled away.

I didn't throw him out. Not that night anyway. We never spoke for several days; he avoided me like the plague. Whilst I had got a shock when Lee disclosed his criminal activities, this shock-wave was on a different level. I still loved him. That wouldn't change soon but, as far as I was concerned, this was the ultimate betrayal; the worst thing that any man could do to me.

I returned to the doctor to get checked out. I felt like a cheap street whore. When I walked into the waiting room, it was as though everybody knew why I was there. Why should I feel like that? Why had Lee made me feel that way? It was good news.

"All clear," the doctor told me.

She discussed protection and birth control. I don't think I heard a word she said. I was in another world, a world of torment and torture. The man I loved had ripped my heart out and torn it to pieces. As the weeks passed, I suspected there were more betrayals. I told myself I was paranoid. I so wanted to believe it was a single one-night stand.

When Lee left one day, he forgot to pick up his Filofax. It was his Bible, everything he did with every appointment; every contact was in that Filofax. He had left it in the lounge. I picked it up, took it through to the kitchen and opened it. I flipped past the diary section and the notes; I went straight to contacts. There were almost a hundred contacts and, as I flicked through, I realised I knew most of them. I wasn't interested in the men though, the Dave G and Gary J, the weird nicknames of Quinny, the Dodger and the Rabbi. No, I was only interested in the girls; the girls I didn't know.

There were seventeen girls' names in total. I knew

eleven of them. There were only six girls to call. I walked over to the fridge and opened a bottle of white wine. I poured a large glass and emptied half of it in one gulp. I took a deep breath and called the first one, Samantha.

"Hi," I said. "How are you, Samantha? It's Cookie."

I could hear the confusion on the other end of the line.

"I'm sorry," she said. "Do I know you?"

"Of course you do, darling. I'm Lee's girlfriend."

There was an uncomfortable silence; I could almost hear the cogs of deceit and lies turning in her head.

"I'm sorry," she said. "I think you have the wrong number."

Before I could say another word, she hung up.

"The fucking bitch," I muttered under my breath.

I could sense her guilt. Her number was in his contacts, and she knew exactly who Lee was.

I called Penelope. "Hi Penelope, it's Cookie, Lee's girlfriend."

Penelope didn't even give me the pleasure of a brief discussion. She hung up immediately and then I knew.

I finished my wine and poured another. In a warped sort of way, I was having fun and the alcohol certainly helped. For weeks after I had been to the doctor, my head had been in a state of flux. I didn't know what to think or what to believe. With each girl

I called, the picture was becoming clearer. I called a girl called Sarah and, as soon as I said who I was, she burst into tears and started to apologise. We had a real heart to heart. I couldn't get her off the phone after she told me she was married and begged me not to tell her husband. She said it was all about the sex, how Lee would meet up with her once a week when her husband was out with his mates. I felt sorry for her in the end and promised her I wouldn't tell her husband.

"Please," she said. "I promise I'll end it right this minute. I'll call him right now."

I told her not to bother; I said there were at least another five girls he was fucking regularly. That shocked her. Just like me, she thought she was the only one. Just for the hell of it, I telephoned the other three. It was the same story for two of them apart from a girl called Louise, who turned out to be a cousin of Lee's that he had never talked about.

I finished the bottle of wine. Lee came home just after ten. I threw his Filofax at him and then my empty glass. I went to bed. But, I had a plan. I wanted to get away from him; I needed to think about my future; I didn't know at the time whether my plans would include Lee.

I had dipped in and out of the modelling business and, although it paid well, it was sporadic with no long-term contracts on the horizon. I decided I would fly out to Barbados. I knew a few models there that were doing well with a couple of agencies. It was one of the places to be seen in and I knew I had the figure and the height these agencies were looking for.

When I told Lee of my intentions, he begged me not to go. But, I bought a one-way ticket and accepted a lift when he offered to drop me at the airport.

"When are you coming back?" he asked.

"I really don't know, Lee."

"That's not fair, babe."

I glared at him. "Don't you dare talk to me about fair."

As the British Airways flight took off from Gatwick, I genuinely didn't know when I would be back. I watched from my window seat as London gradually disappeared and I shed a few tears. I realised I had to cut Lee adrift. Homer had been right all along. Oh, how I wished I had listened to him when he had tried to warn me. Lee was bad news. He was a criminal and a serial cheat.

* * *

Barbados was all I hoped it would be. I worked hard, turned up at anything and everything and got regular, well-paid modelling work. I didn't delete Lee's number from my phone book, but I had clarified that it was over and told him to find someone else who would put up with his infidelity.

I hadn't told him where I was staying. Why should I? This was my chance to get him out of my life once and for all. But then the letters arrived. I couldn't understand how he got my address, one a week, then three and four, each one begging me to come back. Occasionally, he would send a tape-recorded message professing his undying love for me, telling me how he had changed, how he would never put his friends before me again and how he had made the biggest mistake of his life in an intoxicated stupor of drink and drugs.

I didn't respond at first. Why should I? I may well have forgiven him for one slip up. I cared for him that much, but he had had at least six women on the go and I couldn't handle that. He loved me more than life itself, he had said. He could change and claimed that he had never slept with a woman since he waved goodbye to me at Gatwick. As the months slipped by, I think he got the picture. He was no longer sending me as many letters or recorded messages, twice a month at the most.

What he didn't know, and I didn't tell him, was that Mick Jagger had asked me out on a date. I had been on the island for a few months when I heard Mick had arrived. It was the cricket season. The world cup and the West Indies were at the top of their game, as were England. It was the game everyone wanted to see and, of course, the press had announced just how big a cricket fan Mick Jagger was.

I attended the match with a group of friends. It was so unlike watching cricket in the UK. There were BBQs and music, lots of dancing, cool boxes full of beer and rum punch. People were there to have a good time. The cricket match was incidental to the fun, and the atmosphere was electrifying. My friends and I were in the grandstand, with a superb view of the complete match and that's when I saw him. I turned around at half time and Mick Jagger was standing there, just a few yards away, on his own. He smiled, so I approached him and introduced myself. Why the hell not? I wanted a picture with him. I was wearing a tight, revealing top in mango orange with baggy white trousers and revealing a bare midriff. Mick said I looked cool.

We talked for a while and watched most of the match together before he asked me for my number. I got a couple of photos with him and thought that would be the last I ever heard from him. The West Indies won the match and the World Cup and, wouldn't you know? Mick invited me to the VIP party! I met all the players; I made sure I got all their signatures on a mini cricket bat for my brother.

Mick called me the next day and I asked if I'd like to go out to dinner that evening. He said he was at Eddie Grant's recording studio laying down some tracks. I said yes and he asked for my address. A chauffeur came to pick me up at eight o'clock that evening.

We drove through the darkness to Eddie Grant's house on the North Coast of the island. It hosted incredible recording studio and tennis courts. Mick was there, but we didn't stay too long. It was getting late by the time we reached the Crane Beach hotel for dinner. The kitchen was about to close when we arrived and the dining room was practically empty but don't you know that if Mick Jagger wanted dinner, then they would be happy to stay open a little longer. We had the fish and talked most of the evening. Poor guy, I kind of interrogated him about how he got into music and about modelling. I was there for one reason, I wanted tips on how to make it in the music and modelling industry. I loved singing and he was the best person to give me that advice. He said at first, people wanted the Rolling Stones to be more like other bands but that they had a unique sound and weren't going to change for anyone. It was their uniqueness that made them famous in the end.

Mick was the perfect gentleman. As his chauffeur turned up to drive me home, he said, "Do what you do best and don't let anyone persuade you to change."

Wise words.

I was in Barbados for six months when I had the big break I was hoping for. An agent from Valentino, Italy, had approached me after a photo shoot in Bridgetown Bay. He said I had the look they were searching for and invited me to Milan. I doubted him at first. The modelling industry is full of men who promise the earth and then don't deliver. Worse, there are scammers out there who charge young girls thousands of dollars for portfolio shoots with no prospect of any work at the end.

I sat down with the man over a drink. "So, you want me to come to Milan?"

"Yes."

"And how much will that cost me?"

He reached into his man bag and handed me an envelope. "This is a flight ticket to Milan. We want you to be our in-house model for the Milano Spring Fashion Show."

I swallowed hard.

He continued. "It's a one-way ticket because there are later shows in Japan and New York and we want you at both of them."

He handed me another envelope. "There's ten thousand dollars in there for expenses. That should last you a month or two and by then we'll have your contract sorted out."

I couldn't speak. This man wasn't playing games.

I took the envelope and looked inside. It was full of one hundred American dollar bills.

"We have given you US dollars because it's easier to change into other currency denominations and the dollar is strong."

"Thank you," I said. "I don't know what to say."

"Just tell me you will be on the flight."

"Yes, of course I will."

As I walked away, I was floating on air. I had made it. This was what I had been working towards for the six months I had been in Barbados. I had survived without Lee and knew that if I could survive six months, I could survive a lifetime.

9

AN OFFER I COULDN'T REFUSE

I had to go back to London before my modelling career took off. There were things to do, domestic and housekeeping bits and pieces to tie up, bills to settle, that sort of thing. I couldn't have been more excited as when I called Lee to tell him about how wonderful my new life was going to be, albeit without him. He seemed strangely subdued, quieter than I he had been for a long time.

"I'll meet you at the airport," he said.

"No, honestly, it's fine, I'll—"

I told him we both needed to move on. It would be better if I took a cab.

He wouldn't hear of it. Despite my objections, I found myself blabbing the details of my flight and, as the thought of seeing him again ran through my head, those familiar chemical reactions began to bubble up deep within me.

The flight landed at around six in the morning. It had taken nearly nine hours and all that time I had been talking to myself about my relationship with Lee.

It was over, I'd said to myself. *Remember, we are just friends.*

That was blown out of the water as soon as I saw him standing at the gate; he broke out into a huge smile as soon as he saw me.

I was shaking like a leaf.

What the fuck is wrong with you? I asked myself. *Get a grip, lady.*

"You look gorgeous," he whispered before he kissed me on the lips. I offered no resistance.

I felt fit and toned; I was tanned and glowing from the Caribbean sun, unlike those from a grey and overcast England.

It's difficult to describe my feelings towards Lee at that precise point. While I still carried a little anger, I think I had forgiven him for his infidelity and it felt strange to kiss him, or any man, after so long. I hadn't even looked at a man during the six months I had been in Barbados. Six months without kissing or any type of sexual activity is a long time for anyone, or at least it was for me. As we drove off, his gorgeous, manly, musky smell and expensive aftershave permeated the atmosphere and memories, especially the sexual ones, filled my mind. Although I tried to tell myself I was in control, I knew I had to have him.

Lee appeared calm; there were no visible signs that he felt the same way I did. He remained cool and said all the right things. He had missed me; he told me once again that he had never looked at another woman for six months. I gave him more details about my new career and how we couldn't hold down any sort of relationship if I was on the other side of the world. He said he understood. I told him that, although I felt I had forgiven him, I hadn't forgotten about what he had done to me. He said he understood that too.

We headed straight to his mum's house. He told me he was a reformed character; he had given up a lot of his old ways and had moved back in with his mum because he needed a stabilising influence. I loved his mum. She was a jolly, friendly woman who always had a smile and made me feel so welcome. She had a grin on her face when she saw me and welcomed me home like a long-lost daughter; all the while she was casting a glance or two between Lee and me.

"He's missed you so much, Cookie. I always knew that you were perfect for one another."

Before I could object to her remark or tell her how my life was going to pan out without her son, she announced that my favourite dish was just about ready. The smell of curried goat hung in the air. She'd made fried dumplings too (at bloody breakfast time!) and I realised how hungry I was.

After we had eaten, his mum told us she had to go

out for some shopping.

She looked at Lee and winked. "You two have a lot of catching up to do."

No, I wanted to say, *this will not happen. We are just good friends.*

As soon as his mum left, we looked at each other and we both knew there was only one thing on our minds. We headed straight to his bedroom and started kissing passionately as he unbuttoned my blouse and I tore his shirt off.

"We can't," I said. "I'm not on the pill."

As he dropped his trousers to the floor, he told me not to worry. "I won't come inside you; you won't get pregnant."

He could have told me the sky was green with pink clouds and I would have believed him, I was desperate for him, I just needed to feel that electricity, that fire between us that transcends life on this earth, and I sincerely believed he would follow through with the plan.

It would never happen; we couldn't get enough of each other. He came far too quickly and couldn't stop himself, not that I was in any fit state to even care at that point. And yet when I realised what he had done I was furious.

"What are you doing?" I yelled. "I told you I didn't want to get pregnant; I am not on the bloody pill!"

He apologised profusely as I stomped around yelling at him for not following the plan. He took me in his arms and kissed me gently and before I knew it, the sexual urges had resurfaced and we were back in bed again – *making up.*

He lasted longer this time. I was in sexual heaven as I realised how much I had missed him, and yes, how much I still loved him with all my heart. It had taken less than an hour before all the old feelings had been rekindled.

He came inside me again. He apologised, but I didn't care at this point.

Why am I so weak? I wondered.

We made love another twice before his mum returned. I convinced myself that it was very unlikely I would get pregnant anyway. We had accidentally slipped up on several occasions in the past and nothing had happened. Why should it be any different this time?

I went home to my dad's house and made arrangements to travel to Italy. Despite realising that I was still in love with Lee, I couldn't wait for my new adventure to begin. I had to get over there as early as possible, before the August break, and I needed to make a name for myself.

Lee and I discussed our relationship; we both agreed how much we had missed each other and how much in love we were. The past was the past, we agreed. We were younger then and everyone was entitled to one mistake. I still wanted to go through with my Italian adventure. It could set us up for life and Lee said he backed me one hundred percent.

He took me to the airport again, and we said goodbye. It was very emotional because, although at that point we were very much back together and I knew I could never stop loving him, I wondered if I could ever trust him. I wanted to throw myself into my new career and see what happened. A long-distance relationship wasn't ideal but, if we could still love each other and be faithful as I travelled the globe, then surely we could stand the test of time. The last thing he said to me as I left for the departures gate was that he would never let me down again.

"Promise?" I asked.

"I've never been so certain of anything in my entire life."

He held me tight as I kissed him, never wanting to let him go. And yet I was confused. I was in floods of tears as I walked away. Yes, I loved him and I couldn't get enough of him but, deep down, I still knew that he was no good, trouble with a capital T and, as far as marriage, babies and him being a father figure was concerned, he was a million light-years away from the ideal man I had conjured up in my mind. I shrugged off my feelings.

He can change, I told myself.

The epicentre of fashion and style is Italy, and I was excited. I was determined to become fluent in Italian. I loved everything about the country and the culture, the food, the sense of style and I was sure it would live up to my expectations, despite missing Lee and the sex. I can honestly say I was never interested in another man. The Italian men were different from what I'd known before, very confident and forward. Every man who passed me said the same thing, *Ciao Bella*, which meant that they thought I was gorgeous.

What is wrong with these men? I thought.

I hadn't experienced that in the UK. Although I liked the attention at first, it soon became annoying because I couldn't go out for a casual drink without getting mobbed by men with their tongues hanging out. In the end, I stopped going out! It was as if they had never seen a woman before. However, if the truth be told, they were cute, but my mind was always on Lee.

We had arranged a time of day to phone each other and I stuck to it like glue. My life revolved around those phone calls and nothing got in the way. Not so for Lee, it appeared. Once or twice he wasn't there at our arranged time and his mum would answer; she said he was working but that she would give him the message to be around when I called back. I accepted it and knew that he couldn't phone me because there was no phone at my apartment in Italy.

I shared with two other girls from London. One was from West London and the other was of mixed race from Dagenham. Back home, her mother looked after her eleven-month-old baby; I couldn't help thinking how good she looked considering she had given birth, not even a year before.

We all shared the same dream, and that was to

make a career in Italy, the pinnacle of the fashion world. I was the only one working for Valentino. The other two had auditioned, but they were told their thighs were too fat and had to slim down. I was lucky... I could eat whatever I wanted and never put on any weight. I was a size eight, and that was it. My flatmates bitched and joked that I would end up being a size sixteen as I ate cream cakes by the dozen. I never put on an ounce. It positively killed them.

I had only been in Italy for about three weeks when I did one particular fashion show. It was good except the sound system didn't work, so we had to walk out without music but I imagined a tune in my head and carried it off perfectly. The owner approached me after the show; he was so pleased and appreciative of what I had done. In his late thirties, he was suntanned and handsome and said by way of a thank-you that he would like to pick me up and take me out to dinner in Verona on the banks of Lake Garda, next to a house once owned by Mussolini. I was thrilled and was sure it was all above board. He picked me up in his red Ferrari and took me to what was considered the best restaurant in town. As soon as we sat down and he ordered the most expensive champagne on the menu, I thought there might be an ulterior motive. Sure enough, mid-way through the main course, he came out with it.

"I have big plans for you, Cookie, I would like you to travel with me to the South of France and Monaco in the summer," he said. "I have a villa there, you can stay with me."

I was shocked; there was no doubt at what he was suggesting. He went on to say that he had been divorced for three years; he hadn't dated for a while but now felt that the time was right to start again. He reached across and stroked my hand. I thanked him very much for his kind offer, said I was flattered he thought that way about me but proceeded to tell him about my wonderful boyfriend in London.

He asked what Lee did, then told me he could offer the things that Lee couldn't. Money didn't influence me, nor did promises of exotic travel. I stopped short of telling him about Lee's criminal activities, that he was into property, which was a sort of half-true. I didn't explain that it was other people's property he was into, normally under the cover of darkness, without their consent.

I declined his offer politely, he didn't seem too put out and I guessed it was all in a day's work for someone so influential, so rich, with beautiful models at his beck and call. I dare say a fair few of them even shared his bed, figuring that it wouldn't do their careers any harm.

10

SURPRISE, SURPRISE

The following month, my period hadn't come. I never really took much notice of dates, but I had gone back on the pill after my trip to London and with the pill, you don't lose track. I had the pain but no period. At first, I put it down to stress and the new environment, but it was a strange feeling. I told the girls of my concerns and we got a home testing kit. The result was negative. That was a relief. The last thing I needed in my life was a baby. I convinced myself that I'd have my period in a day or two.

A week later, we arranged a girl's trip to Venice, but I still hadn't had my period. I knew something wasn't right, but assured myself that pregnancy tests didn't lie. I'd been to the dress fitter a few days prior and she had measured my waist. I could understand parts of the Italian conversation when she told her assistant something about my waist being big.

I replied in Italian that it was not true; my waist was twenty-four inches as it had always been. But I didn't carry a tape measure with me and she had measured me. She shook her head, insinuating that she was never wrong and her tape measure never lied. I tried the clothes on that I had to wear for a show and they fitted me perfectly so I gave her that 'I told you so look' and she walked away muttering under her breath.

And yet, I was feeling tired all the time. As soon as I sat in a chair, I'd fall asleep, even in the middle of the afternoon. That was so unlike me; something was going on. In a restaurant one night, I had ordered a blue steak, even though I normally preferred them well done. The steak was so succulent it was perfect, and I couldn't get enough of it as the blood and the juices mingled in my mouth. I thought I had died and gone to heaven; the taste was exquisite.

On the morning of a trip to Venice, we had to get up early to catch the train to the city. I was still concerned about not having my period and had bought another home testing kit, just in case. As soon as I woke up, I went into the bathroom to use it. I sat on the toilet and waited for the little blue line. Within a few seconds, there it was. Fuck! I was pregnant.

I said nothing to the other girls at first. I needed time to process what I had discovered and, although I was in shock, a part of me was quite thrilled. We travelled from Milan by train and when we got to Venice, it looked as beautiful as it did in every painting and travel brochure I had ever seen.

I was overwhelmed by the ambiance of the place, it was so peaceful despite the crowds and, as we crossed the bridge into the main square, it seemed the right place to tell them I was pregnant. They squealed with delight. I joined in and it was the perfect setting under the circumstances to announce such a life-changing event. We took in a few of the sites and talked incessantly about motherhood and what that might mean. By late afternoon, we were hungry and the girls insisted on an upmarket pizza restaurant. But, not me. I wanted potatoes, nothing but potatoes, boiled potatoes, jacket potatoes, chips or mash, as long as it was potatoes. The cravings had started!

When the excitement of the trip died down and we returned to Milan, my thoughts turned to what I would do next. I knew I had to tell Lee but I didn't want to do it over the phone. And then there was my modelling career, how would I tell my employers and what would their reaction be? I notified them within twenty-four hours and, strangely enough, they were quite okay with it. After all, I was hardly the first model to get pregnant. They said they were quite happy to wait for me and I could return after the baby was born.

I booked a flight to London and rang Lee. He wasn't expecting me back; I told a little white lie and said the company had given me a week off because they'd won some sort of fashion award. I went to the market and bought a pair of yellow knitted booties. This was how I was going to tell him. I had it all worked out, I'd wrap them up and give them to him, watch his face as the penny dropped. I also bought him a Stockwell Flight watch with a glass back that showed all the workings as a gift for the new dad. I couldn't wait to get home and tell him. The watch cost as much as I had earned that month, but I didn't care because I was making good money, and anyway, my man was worth every penny.

He picked me up from the airport. As soon as I got into his car, he announced that he had a court hearing and was worried he was going to get banged up.

I sighed deeply. "You told me you had left that sort of thing behind."

"I have," he said. "This is something that happened a long time ago and it's only just caught up with me."

"And you've left the other girls behind too?"

He smiled. He smiled that long deep smile of his and, as I looked into his eyes, he leaned in and kissed me. "You know I have, babe, a promise is a promise."

I was so excited; I couldn't wait a second longer. He turned on the ignition and was ready to pull away, but I told him to switch off the engine.

"Why?"

"Because I have something for you."

I produced the watch. It was special and he knew it. His eyes lit up and a smile crept across his face.

"It's magnificent, a Stockwell Flight watch. My God, I love it," he said.

I turned it over. "Look at the back."

I showed him the glass cover and the small ruby that could be seen in the centre. He kissed me long and hard. This was my man and we were in love. I couldn't have been happier.

He broke the kiss and quizzed me. "But it's not my birthday. Why have you bought it?"

"I have something else to show you," I said

I told him to close his eyes. "Put your hands out."

"Babe, we have to get going. Stop playing games."

"Do as I say."

"Okay."

He closed his eyes and put his hands out. I reached into the bag and took out the booties, leaned over and laid them in his hands.

"Open your eyes."

I watched his face as he opened his eyes and looked down. It took a few seconds to focus and realise what he was holding, and why.

He lifted his head and looked at me. Again, a smile spread across his face and a tremendous surge of relief coursed through my veins. It could have gone either way; you never know how a man is going to react to that news.

I nodded without saying a word.

He broke the silence. "You're pregnant?"

"Yes, your bloody mistake," I joked.

He trembled as his mouth fell open and for a few

seconds before he leaned across and hugged me. He held me tighter than he had ever held me before.

"That's fantastic," he said. "I'm going to be a father; you're going to be a mum!"

"I think that's how it works," I teased.

He kissed me again.

I whispered in his ear, "I love you so much."

"Me too," he replied.

And I *did* love him. I loved him with every fibre of my being.

The entire way home, I was on the air. I swear it was the happiest I had ever been in my life. I was day-dreaming about where we would live, nurseries and colour schemes. I was also thinking up boys' and girls' names. I'd be the perfect mum; we'd push the pram together, a mum and a dad going for long walks and holidays by the seaside.

"I need to get some cigarettes," he announced as he slowed the car down and stopped at the corner shop. He had the watch on and kept looking at it as he got out of the car. I could see that he liked it.

"You'll have to cut out that habit when the baby comes along," I said before he closed the door. "We don't want our son or daughter breathing that shit in."

"We'll see," he said.

I pulled the passenger sun blind towards me and looked in the mirror. Damn... my eye shadow was smudged. I rummaged in my bag for a tissue, but all I could find was an empty packet. I looked around the car. Nothing. I stretched forward and opened the glove compartment. There was nothing there, no tissues. There was a leather folder with his car documents and I pulled that out to see if there were some tissues right at the back. I couldn't see anything and stretched a little further and, as I fumbled blindly, my hand located something. I gripped it and pulled it out. The box was in the palm of my hand. My heart pounded in my chest as my eyes focussed on the writing. *Durex. Pack of twelve.*

I don't know why, but I opened the box. I still trusted him. These condoms were for me, I told myself; at last he had taken on some sort of responsibility. My hopes were dashed a split second later. There were only four condoms left, the rest of the box was stuffed full of empty foil packets.

The sense of betrayal was instant and a hundred times worse than the last time he had betrayed me because now I was pregnant with his child. It shattered my dreams in seconds. It was as if someone had plunged a dozen daggers into my heart. There would be no house, no father, and no happy family home.

I had been brought up by a single parent and I knew how hard that was on both the parent and the child. It wasn't how I saw my future, and it certainly wasn't the future I wanted for my baby. I felt sick to the stomach and my head spun; tears welled up in my eyes. How could he do this to me?

As soon as he came back into the car, I exploded. "What the fuck have you been up to? You told me those days were over."

Before he could answer, I burst into tears. I just couldn't believe my stupidity. I was so angry with myself for being so weak that I had fallen for all his lies and promises. He tried to speak, but I was done with anything he said.

"Don't even fucking begin to try and talk yourself out of this one because you're a liar and anything that comes out of your mouth is pure bullshit."

"But, babe... I—"

"Take me to my dad's right now."

We drove in silence for the last few minutes to my dad's while I wiped the tears from my cheeks with the back of my hand. Lee sat in the car while I stormed round to take my suitcase out of the boot. I didn't look back as I walked up the path to the door; he drove off. I stood there for some minutes and tried to compose myself. I put on a brave face at home; I didn't want my father to know what had been going on.

As I climbed the stairs to my bedroom, I suddenly remembered the watch and I wanted it back. I was fuming; thoughts of revenge were swimming around my head. I had never been so angry in my life and the tears of hurt and sorrow gave way to fury. I genuinely wanted to kill him. How dare he do this to me and my unborn child? I didn't waste much time. I formulated a plan and put it into practice within the hour. I knew his friends and made some phone calls. I told them about the watch I had just brought back from Italy and said I would sell it to them at the right price. I mentioned how much it had cost me in Italy and that it was so much cheaper than in the UK. I got a few bites, three of his friends said they would take a look at it.

Then I called Lee. "I'll be round to the house in thirty minutes. I don't want to speak to you; I just want the watch back with the box."

I slammed the phone down and within ten minutes, my cab had arrived. As I walked through my dad's kitchen, I picked up the biggest knife I could find and placed it deep into my handbag. I stormed into Lee's house without even knocking on the door.

I found him in the lounge and demanded the watch back. He took it off his wrist and handed it over without saying a word. His shamefaced look told me he knew he had done wrong and wasn't going to argue with me. That in itself reminded me he had no intention of denying it, he was guilty as charged, no question about it.

I found his car parked at the bottom of the street. It was an Italian vintage car, maybe a replica, an OSCA 1600 GT COUPÉ in light blue; his pride and joy. But not for long. I took out the knife and stabbed it as far as I could into one of the front tyres. "Who the fuck do you think you are?" I muttered to myself as I attacked the other front tyre with a vengeance. The knife was hard to get in, the tyres were rock hard, but the knife was sharp and I gouged a six-inch tear in the second one. "You fucking... cheating... bastard!"

I slashed the two back tyres too and momentarily thought about keying the metallic paintwork for good measure, but the car was too pretty for that. I stood back and looked at my handiwork; each tyre had deflated. I wished that I had picked up a hammer from dad's house because I so wanted to smash every one of his fucking windows. By now I was exhausted, it's hard work slashing four tyres with a kitchen knife, but I felt vindicated. I caught a bus and left before anyone could report me to the police. Lee would know exactly who had vandalised his car but there was no way on earth he would report it.

I went straight to his friend's house. I knew him as Meataxe; he was named, so I heard, after an incident that involved a meat cleaver and some poor guys unfortunate's head. Meataxe was tall and ugly, but we got on well. I got on with all of Lee's dodgy friends. I had placed the watch back into the box and showed it to him. He could see it was brand new, and I told him I had brought it back for Lee, but we'd had an argument, so I just wanted to sell it.

"I love it," he said. "How much do you want for it?"

"It cost me three and a half grand, but if you've got three grand cash, you can have it."

He smiled. "It's a deal, a bargain at that price."

He disappeared upstairs and returned a few minutes later as he counted out three thousand pounds in used notes. As I left Meataxe's house, I had no regrets. I felt better that Lee didn't have something I had bought from a misplaced feeling of love and loyalty. I convinced myself he didn't deserve it.

But a few days later, a wave of depression set in. I was pregnant by a man who I no longer wanted to set eyes on. I was carrying the child of a serial cheat, a liar. How the hell had I wound up in such a mess and what was I going to do? Abortion was the obvious answer, but was out of the question. I didn't believe in abortion. I could never take the life of an unborn child.

Several weeks passed and Lee telephoned me every day. Each time I let the phone go to voicemail, but he never left a message. The thought of talking to him sickened me; I didn't want to hear his voice. He had said a lot of nice things to me in the past. I had believed everything. But now I knew they were just that... words... hollow and toxic.

11

NO FIXED ABODE

There were days when I struggled to get out of bed. He had betrayed me and I was determined to break it off completely, but no switch in the body says 'fall out of love'. I told myself that each day would be a little easier, it wouldn't hurt so much, but it was weeks, even months, before I could walk out of the house and have a conversation with a friend or a neighbour without bursting into tears. I hid it well from my dad. He knew we had split up, but not the exact reason why. I didn't have the heart to tell him. I said we had drifted apart and had called it a day.

My emotions were all over the place, as were my hormones. One day I would walk out of the house feeling stupid and cheap and other days I was wracked with anger and rage and I hated every man I bumped into. And of course, there's the emotion that all women go through when someone has cheated on them, the feeling of worthlessness, of somehow believing it was your fault. You ask yourself questions. Why? What is wrong with me? Others thinking, there must be something wrong with you for your man to do what he did.

I shouldn't have gone to Italy, no wonder he has been unfaithful. I've been selfish and put my career first, leaving my man behind, I let these thoughts go round and round in my head.

But the feelings didn't last long because deep down I knew that no woman could have given more to their man, no girl could have loved someone any more than I did. I took each day as it came and built up my mental toughness. I would be a mum in a few months; there was no time to mope around and feel sorry for myself. I needed to work, find somewhere to live and, most importantly, have a car. There was no way I was going to be one of those mums who struggled with a buggy on and off public transport. No, I was going to provide my child with everything he or she needed.

I had the three thousand pounds from the watch sale and about another five that I had managed to save in Italy. It was a good start; I wasn't exactly penniless.

A new sense of focus was what I found. I started to read the Bible again, something I hadn't done since school, and drew strength from the verses and proverbs. I got a job in the West End as a temp and started to plan my life without Lee.

As I was pregnant and of no fixed abode, I was technically homeless and a friend told me I was entitled to a council flat. I went to the local authority and the receptionist confirmed that she had put me at the top of the waiting list.

"Great," I smiled. "How long will it take?"

She shrugged her shoulders. "It just depends when something suitable comes up."

"Which will be how long?"

"Six to twelve months."

That wasn't what I wanted to hear.

I made a decision that I didn't want to touch the money I had in reserve; that would be for when the baby arrived. I worked hard. I took every hour the agency threw at me and saved most of my wages to put towards a car. I never went out; I lived the life of a hermit.

The feelings of anger towards Lee dampened down. He was the father of my child and would have a right to see his son or daughter. I pushed the feelings of hurt into the deepest recesses of my mind and tried to be practical. My child would need a father figure and Lee had responsibilities for paying for food and clothes and the fixtures and fittings for a nursery, toys, Christmas and birthday presents. I accepted I would need to call Lee sooner rather than later and discuss those sorts of things.

I didn't show until about five months, as my stomach muscles were strong. Because I was glowing but not showing, I was getting a lot of male attention.

One day on the tube coming back from work, a very cute and handsome man named Patrick gave me his number. "Let's meet for a drink," he had said. He lived in Brixton. I was between break ups and it couldn't hurt. *What's good for the goose is good for the gander*, I thought, so I met him at a cocktail bar. He was very handsome and had beautiful eyes with long curled eyelashes, the kind that women spend a fortune to replicate. I dated Patrick. I liked the attention; here was someone who was actually interested in me. As the weeks went by, I knew it could never work. I was pregnant and at some point soon I would need to tell him. I broke it off, making up some random excuse. Although it disappointed him, he didn't fight me.

"If you ever change your mind," he said, "you know where to find me."

Commuting was getting harder as the pregnancy progressed and one day I fainted on the tube. I could feel it coming. It was hot, packed and there were no seats. Three youths had found seats and I looked at them with pleading eyes. I was clearly pregnant. My bump wasn't exactly small. They looked over and laughed at something one of them had said. That annoyed me and I was just about to remonstrate with them when my head spun and my knees buckled. When I came round, I was sitting on a seat by the platform with a small crowd surrounding me.

"Shall we call an ambulance?" someone asked.

"No, I'm fine; I'll call someone to collect me."

I called Lee and told him what had happened and, in a flash, he was at the station. He must have broken every speed limit possible to get there in such a short time.

He took me to where he had parked and helped me in. On the way home, he apologised and we agreed to meet again to talk things over. I told him I needed money for food and transport and he gave it to me. That helped me to save my wages to buy a car. We started seeing each other again but I wasn't going to let him fool me a third time. Before the baby came, I made sure I had a car and I was soon to get a flat.

During my whole pregnancy, since the first initial euphoria of Lee and I having a baby, things between us went back into the usual routine of him paying loads of attention for a week or two, then going missing for days on end. Once again, we had an on/off relationship about half a dozen times during my pregnancy. I hoped he would at last become the man who would be there for our baby and me, not some fly-by-night waste of a man.

When he called during an 'off' time, I refused to answer. I had a renewed fortitude in resistance since seeing Patrick, in fact, every time I broke up with Lee I thought of calling Patrick but I never did. I resigned myself to the fact that, despite everything I had said about not wanting to be a single parent, I had to get on with it. I refused to buy maternity clothes, I was slim and figured I would just buy bigger normal clothes, and I did just that. I went to the anti-natal classes and learned everything I could from books about being a new mum.

Over time, my resistance to Lee's attempts to get back with me waned. When speaking to his friends I'd ask how he was doing and they would always say the same, "He won't admit it but he's missing you." This went on for a few weeks and eventually when the phone rang at midnight one night I knew it was him and I answered.

"Hello."

"It's me. Lee."

"Who?" I said, pretending not to have heard

"Lee, you know, the father of your child."

Damn it, I thought. *How come he always knows what to say?*

"What do you want?" I was melting inside.

"I want to see you."

I said nothing

"Can I come round?"

"No. I'm tired and just about to go to bed."

"Come on, I just want to talk. I won't stay long, promise."

I continued to resist, but inside me every fibre of my being was saying, 'Yes.'

Eventually, I gave in. "Okay, only for a short while. The baby and I need sleep."

I expected him to come over within minutes. That's how much I wanted to see him, but it was a whole half an hour before he knocked on the door.

I wanted to look tired, so I took off my makeup

and wore my dressing gown so that I looked like I was ready for bed. I wasn't going to be so easily manipulated this time.

"Will this take long?" I asked as I opened the door. "I'm exhausted."

He made hot chocolate for us.

That's an improvement, I thought.

"I've been thinking," he said, "about you, the baby and my future. You know it was never supposed to be like this and I know I only have myself to blame. I've been such a fool and I really am truly sorry."

I knew better than to interrupt.

"It's all been a bit sudden, you know; you, me, everything and I really do want to make things right between us, even if you won't have me back. There's no one who means as much to me as you do. I swear on my mother's life."

He loves his mum a lot, so this must be serious, I thought.

"You know I love you; my mother loves you, my dad loves you, all my friends love you and I've been a fool. I think it was the shock, but I know I've gone too far this time and if I could go back in time, I wouldn't make the same mistake again. I know you don't believe me, but it's true."

At that point, he lifted his head and looked me straight in the eyes. I could feel the tears welling up inside me. He lowered his head again. At that moment, all I wanted was to hug him and feel his strong soft arms around me and that spiritual connection I felt deep inside. But I had responsibilities. It wasn't just me anymore; I had our baby to think about. So I said nothing and kept looking down too, trying everything I could to fight the feelings inside.

After a very long pause, I responded. "I need a man I can rely on, Lee, someone who is there for me and the baby, someone who will love us and put us first. I don't think you're that man."

As the words tumbled out of my mouth, my voice broke and tears rolled down my face. I wanted him to be that person, but inside I knew he would never step into those shoes. I told him to go and walked towards the door. He said I was right. I opened the door and he was gone.

He called the next day, and we had a chat, nothing specific, just practical things like the baby's due date and how I was feeling now that I was getting bigger. Lucky for me from behind, I didn't look pregnant. My bump was all in the front. I was feeling tired too; I had no energy, which was very unlike me. He called again that evening at about eight o'clock and asked if he could bring a Chinese takeaway. I agreed, but only on condition that he was away by midnight.

By now, I was eight months pregnant, and I was staying in accommodation provided to expectant mothers who were homeless. An Asian lady and her English lady friend ran it. I had to swear an affidavit to get on the housing list and they put me in a nice bed-and-breakfast halfway house on the edge of the river Thames with several other expectant mothers. Lee could stay over too. The room was decent enough and in the morning; we had breakfast in the dining room.

Lee came over every night for the next two weeks. There was no physical contact between us. We played dominos one night, blackjack the next, watched TV and films, and I never let my guard down. He wasn't spending time with his friends. Lee kept his promise. He had changed. He seemed more serious, and I wanted to believe he was not the same person who had let me down dozens of times before. Slowly but surely, he regained my confidence and I let him back into my life.

When my dad called one day from the Caribbean to make sure everything was okay, I told him I was involved with Lee again. It did not impress him. "You can't make a silk purse from a sow's ear," he warned.

But things were looking up. Lee was coming to visit me every day and we became closer. It was a leap year and Valentine's Day was approaching. Although every brain cell in my head was yelling, he's no good, he's only going to hurt you. Yet every fibre of my body was in love with him again. It was a constant battle between my head and my heart and, with Lee, my heart always won through. His smile, his charismatic personality, his presence; it was all too overwhelming for me to resist. He knew exactly what to say and when to say it and how to say it to get me back. Something addicted me to him.

I had heard that on Valentine's Day, during a leap year, it was traditional for women to ask men to marry them. I liked the idea of that, and I certainly would not miss this opportunity. Having a child without being married was something I had never envisaged. Nice girls don't do that, and as far as I was concerned I was a nice girl. Marriage wasn't something I was going to take lightly. It was an enormous commitment, a commitment for life. I wanted my child to have the perfect family, the right start in life. I believed in the sanctity of marriage. I knew in my heart of hearts that I would never betray my husband and that, by being married, I hoped Lee would stand up to his responsibilities and, as he heard the words of the marriage service, everything would fall into place and we would live happily ever after.

At least that was the plan.

I brought a large Valentine's card for 14th February, the kind that needs a cardboard envelope and inside I wrote – TO MY DARLING LEE, THE LOVE OF MY LIFE, WILL YOU MARRY ME…

I left it where he would literally bump into it on Valentine's Day morning, on the bedside table. I went downstairs. He was notorious for getting up late and this morning was no exception. He was fully dressed and on the way out the door when I asked him about the card.

"Oh yes, I couldn't miss it." He gave me a hug and a kiss.

"And about the proposal?" I said,

"Oh that, no I'm far too young to get married."

I was furious. "But not too young to get me pregnant though, are you?"

"Don't be offended," he said. "You know how it is."

He grinned and then he was gone.

Oh yes, I certainly knew how it was. But the baby's birth was imminent and this was no time to throw a tantrum. By this time, I had found out I was having a boy. The due date for our son came and went and my bump got bigger, so big in fact that I could rest a cup of tea on it when I sat down. My dad returned from his Caribbean trip and, even though I stayed a few nights at his house, he wouldn't let Lee stay over.

I focused on finding a name for our baby and I trawled through dozens of baby books, but nothing seemed quite right. Lee didn't have any ideas. I wanted our son to have a special name. One day, as I was sitting on the top deck of a bus, a voice came to me. It was very clear. "Name him Oscar," it said.

I looked around expecting to see someone sitting behind me but there was no one. It was a weird experience and I'd always said I wanted something a little bit different. When I got home I looked up the meaning it had biblical and Scandinavian connections. Oscar.

Oh well, I thought to myself, *that's it. If we can't think of anything else Oscar will do nicely.*

I was on my own, just after midnight, when my

waters broke. I had just gone to bed and my dad was out visiting his girlfriend. I was petrified and rang him to ask if he could to take me to the hospital. Then I phoned Lee. "I'll see you at the hospital," he said.

Dad took me and left me in the care of the midwives. On the way, I told him that Lee was coming. My dad knew what that meant and left before Lee arrived. We both put on a brave face but I was frightened and so was he. We knew both of our lives were about to change forever. To be honest, neither of us knew what to expect. I had been to the anti-natal classes where they teach you how to breathe, to cope with the pain and I had ordered a tens machine for pain relief, but neither coping mechanism was working for me. As soon as they suggested an epidural, I jumped at it with both hands.

Fourteen hours later, I gave birth to a beautiful baby boy. Oscar was strong and healthy with a full head of shiny black hair and, at birth, had weighed in at 9 pounds (just over 4 kg). A new chapter in our life had begun and I couldn't have been happier.

I remained in hospital for a week as was the norm then and Lee came to visit every day, sometimes alone, other times with our mutual friends. I was the first in the group to have a baby and everyone was excited. My two best friends came with baby clothes and flowers. The nurses helped me change his nappy then bathe him. It was a terrifying first experience, as I feared accidentally drowning him. They showed me how to dress him, how to hold him and all the other skills a new mother needs.

At the end of the week, the local authority had moved me to another place; this one was more like a bedsit in a purpose-built block of flats. It came with central heating so hot you had to open the windows in March; there was an onsite laundry room and a large shared kitchen with utensils. Lee stayed with me all the time and we enjoyed the new experience of being parents together. I remember one day lying on the bed next to Lee and bouncing our son on my stomach, his little legs moving. "Crikey," I said, "he's trying to walk!"

He was only two weeks old, and it scared the hell out of me. I quickly laid him down. No baby walks at two weeks. But our son was a robust baby. His arms and legs were pure muscle, and he was continually trying to move his legs in a walking motion. He wasn't frail but had a presence even at that tender age and unlike all the other babies on the block; he was sleeping most of the night. I felt very lucky. I had a Moses basket next to my bed where he slept soundly, never stirring. He only ever cried when he was hungry.

Things were good between Lee and me at this point, but I still felt wounded, if that's the right word. I think if he had agreed to my marriage proposal and agree to a life with me, I may have been able to put his infidelity behind me and start afresh. I had expected him to commit to me and his new family, but he had thrown it back in my face. That was a deep cut to my heart. I still hadn't given up on the idea of marriage but wouldn't push it. Perhaps Lee just wasn't ready; perhaps he would come round and propose to me in time. I clung to that hope.

12

A BUNDLE OF JOY

Three weeks after Oscar's birth, I was told that permanent accommodation, a council maisonette, had become available. We went to look at it and I couldn't quite believe how beautiful the house and the area were. It was perfect, with two bedrooms and a garden. It was close to the town in a neat little cul de sac.

We moved in a few days later. Everything seemed perfect... but not for long.

Lee's drug business was doing well, but now he was bringing it home. I wasn't having it and I put my foot down and reminded him I wanted nothing to do with his illegal activities. There was only one thing that mattered now, and that was Oscar. It was bad enough that his father was a dealer, but I wasn't turning my son's home into a drug den. I told Lee that if the council found out, they would evict us and I had no intention of making my son homeless.

As always, my relationship with Lee was a rollercoaster of emotions. I loved him so much, but at times, I hated everything he stood for. His relationship with me was the same as his relationship with his son. Occasionally, he would put on an act as if he was the best father in the world and the best partner a girl could wish for. But most times he put his business and friends first, even his drug-ridden clients were placed before us, we were so far down the list it was embarrassing. He would disappear for days on end.

Little Oscar would ask where he was. I'd tell him, "Daddy is working."

Lee would reappear as if it was just normal. I'd ask where he'd been. "Just working," he'd say with a smile.

I focused my attention on my child. Nothing was too good for Oscar. I enrolled him in a Montessori Nursery School just before he was twelve months old. It was a school that believed children are eager for knowledge and capable of learning in a supportive and thoughtfully prepared learning environment. The school believes it can develop the child physically, socially, emotionally, and spiritually. I tried to talk to Lee about how good the school would be for our son.

"Whatever you say, babe," was his normal response.

As Oscar progressed through his schooling, I enrolled him in additional French lessons, horse riding and martial art classes as soon as he was old enough. I was determined that he would have the same opportunities I had in life, if not better, and that he would not turn out anything like his father. He was such a good boy and advanced in everything he did.

Lee appeared to be on a different planet. While I spent all the time and money I had on the development of our son, Lee appeared to be going off in a completely different direction. He threw parties at the house, stayed out until the early hours of the morning and, although I didn't find any evidence that he was cheating on me, he was living the life of a single man again. I told him time and time again he had a son and that came with a level of responsibility.

We argued like crazy and in the end, I told him to leave even though there was a part of me wanted him to stay.

He didn't leave immediately and after a few days I wondered to myself, was there a last chance saloon for us, could he change? No chance! What he did next was simply unbelievable.

Without me knowing, he brought a gun into the house. He had hidden it in the bottom drawer of a cabinet in our bedroom. I walked out of the shower one morning to find him sitting on the bed cleaning it.

I flipped. "What the fuck, Lee? What is that?"

"It's a gun," he said, like he was handling a mobile phone.

I hit the roof.

"Relax," he said. "It's only a gun; Oscar didn't react like this when I showed it to him."

I couldn't believe it. He'd shown the gun to our two-year-old son.

No matter how much I wanted to believe Lee could change, I knew now that he never would. He had an alternative way of living, of earning money and of existing. His style of life entrenched him; we came from two different worlds.

I said nothing, went to the cupboard and took out a roll of black plastic bags. Without speaking, I filled the bags with every piece of his clothing, his shoes and trainers. He looked at the four plastic bags and didn't say a word. One by one, I threw them out of the front door and onto the grass. He got the message and left; I was relieved. I vowed he would never return to my environment. I would never expose my son to his world. I would rather die first.

I made popcorn and Oscar and I watched the Lion King. It was a peaceful day for a change. I had turned a chapter in my life and my son would never know what street life was all about. I'd concentrate on his education, instil morals in him and steer him clear of anybody or anything that represented the dark side.

After we had separated, Lee came round at least once or twice a month using the excuse that he wanted to see Oscar. On those occasions, he was dressed immaculately and on his best behaviour. It was clear he was trying to impress; he wanted me back and told me often enough, but I wasn't interested.

A pattern had developed. Lee adored me from afar, but when we were living together, there was very little affection and care towards me and he spent very little time with Oscar. He took everything for granted. Yet, on the occasions when I kicked him out, he appeared outwardly devastated, telling me and Oscar how much he missed us. He'd come round and make a fuss of Oscar, take him out to the park or the shops and buy him things. It was all so frustrating because I knew deep down how much Lee loved us both. Every time he turned up on the doorstep declaring his undying love for us both, I so wanted to believe he had turned a corner.

But life had changed for me. By this time, I had joined the Pentecostal Church and became a born-again Christian. For once, I felt part of a community again and the church services were like going to a rave. There were lots of singing and dancing. It was awesome and so uplifting, I couldn't get enough of it. My outlook on life had changed. I had transformed my heart and soul with God's spirit. My mind, my will and my emotions had changed, and the church gave me all the love and support I had craved from Lee.

I became heavily involved in the church, which gave me a new perspective on what life was really about. I found peace and tranquillity and could focus on my home, my child and my career, which I was desperately trying to get back on track. A few jobs had come in, but the income limited me. I wasn't earning enough to sustain us or provide the lifestyle I wanted for my son.

I needed a more regular income because I was on my own and Lee was offering little or no financial support. I was more than aware that my son's father was walking a dangerous tightrope and could be caught and jailed at any time. I didn't want to go down with him.

And I didn't even want to contemplate what might happen if he got mixed up with other drug gangs or turf wars. London had had over one hundred murders that year, with the vast majority related to gang warfare linked to drugs.

As chance would have it, I started my own business. I opened a sandwich shop and it went incredibly well. But I wasn't spending sufficient time with Oscar and the hours I had to put in to the shop made it difficult to find someone to look after him. It was clear I needed some other type of work, something that would fit in with my role as a mother and provide me with the income I needed. I was a single parent and didn't I know it.

The business grew, and I was delighted that I had made a success of it but, it became increasingly impossible to continue to sustain the commitment needed for it to survive. The busiest time was over lunch and it wasn't unusual for me to look out at the twenty metre queue outside and wonder how I was going to cope. Friends told me I should expand or even offer the shop out as a franchise but, although these avenues would have brought in more money, I didn't want to think how many more hours it would add to my working day. I didn't have the strength to develop the business further, and I was missing Oscar; I barely saw him for two or three hours a day, and when I did get home, I was physically and mentally shattered.

Eventually, I got an offer that was too good to refuse. It was a relief to sell the business as a going concern, something that gave me enough money to take a well-earned rest and be in a position to spend more time with my son.

We took a holiday together; which gave me time to reflect on what I truly wanted out of life and what was best for Oscar. As much as I fought the urge to take Lee back, I wanted Oscar to grow up in a secure environment with a positive role model and father figure; someone we could both truly love. Above all, I wanted someone who would respect and care for both of us.

I started to date a few guys and I'll be honest, I was looking not just for a mate but a father to my son, I think that was always my first consideration. Oscar came first, my love life and relationships with men were secondary.

13

A CHANGE OF DIRECTION

I had known Pablo for about two years before I was pregnant; we knew each other from the rave scene and he had dated one of my good friends for a while. He was half Brazilian and half Portuguese, very good looking with olive skin, curly black hair. He had the most beautiful brown eyes, as deep as a dark ocean and as mesmerising as a sunrise, and the longest eyelashes I'd ever seen on a man. I got on well with Pablo. We hit it off straight away, but he was never any more than a good friend.

I remember being in Tooting one day visiting Lee and I had stopped off to get a takeaway. Oscar was asleep in his child's seat. I parked right outside the shop and walked in, keeping an eye on the car. I was in the shop for a matter of seconds and when I walked out, I bumped into Pablo. We said hello, and that we hadn't seen each other for a while; he gave me a hug and a kiss on the cheek.

I pointed to the car. "My son, he's asleep."

Pablo looked shocked.

"I didn't know," he said. "Who's his dad?"

"Lee, but we are not together."

"Oh, no!" he said. "What happened?"

"It's a long story."

Pablo walked towards the car and peered into the back seat. I saw the reaction when he set eyes on Oscar. It was as if he'd melted and a big, genuine smile spread across his face.

"He's beautiful."

"I have to agree," I joked.

He lingered for a while. I think he wanted Oscar to wake up, but it wasn't going to happen. He was completely out of it. We said goodbye. I told him we should keep in touch and he said he would like that very much.

A week later, he was on the phone and invited my friends and I to a party.

That night, Pablo acted differently from the way he'd always been with me. Several times I noticed him staring at me and, as we made eye contact, he'd break out into a big smile. Towards midnight, I was standing on my own and he came over. We sat down and talked. He'd had a few drinks but wasn't drunk; the words seemed to tumble from his mouth.

Pablo told me his heart sank when he saw Oscar.

He had always dreamed of being with me one day. It was almost as if it wasn't right that I'd had a child with another man.

"What?" I asked in amazement.

"It's true, Cookie, I've always had feelings for you and I'm glad you have split from Lee."

"Don't say that," I said. "It's not nice."

He shrugged his shoulders; said he couldn't help feeling the way he did and his feelings towards me would always be the same. From then on, I changed towards him. We said goodbye soon after. I wondered if he was going to regret what he had said in the cold light of a sober day.

That wasn't the case, and a few weeks later, he invited me to another party, this time on my own.

The party was in Tooting and I'd be lying if I said I hadn't thought about what Pablo had said at the previous party. When I saw him, I gave him a hug and he kissed me on the cheek again. I felt compelled to hug him a second time. It was like an automatic response and when I did, something inside me moved. We pulled apart. I looked him directly in the eyes and, oh my God, I started to 'fancy' him. It was so strange for me and I was curious why this had happened; in all the time I had known Pablo, I had never felt this way. Suddenly, he was the most attractive man on the planet.

We were together most of the evening. We flirted with each other outrageously but we didn't take it any further. The conversation steered around to my religious beliefs, the church, and how I had become a born-again Christian. Pablo clarified he didn't believe. He said that a church building made him feel uncomfortable.

We had a friendly argument about our different beliefs, but I admired his honesty. He told me he respected my views and could see how passionate I was about God and my church.

He called me the next day.

"How are you?"

"Great, it was a good night."

"What are you doing today?" he asked.

"You've forgotten already, Pablo? It's a Sunday and Oscar and I are off to church in about an hour."

"I thought so," he said. "Do you mind if I tag along?"

"What? You want to go to church?"

"Yes."

"But I thought they made you feel uncomfortable."

"Not if I'm with you."

He'd caught me by surprise, but I agreed. The church was in Tooting, where he lived. "Do you want me to pick you up?"

"That would be great."

It was probably our first proper date and we were in church. I couldn't help seeing the funny side. I was the most spiritual girl on the planet and he was an atheist. You couldn't make it up. And yet it worked and a special wave washed over me because I knew how uncomfortable he was with religion and yet he stood there with me, by my side, it was almost a display of how much he thought of me and my son and it touched me.

I studied Pablo whenever we were together with Oscar. It was clear that he was very fond of him and slowly but surely, I saw him stepping into the father's role, far more in fact than his real father. Lee still turned up occasionally when I was dating Pablo. I think he had probably heard through the grapevine that I had begun dating again and he wouldn't have been comfortable with that, although he didn't come right out and say it.

We met every Sunday and went to church. Pablo even joined in the songs, and I could see that he was getting a lot out of it. After church, we would go for a walk on Tooting Common or Richmond Park, and we'd sit and watch while Oscar played on the swings. We were a normal happy family and, over time, I saw how much Pablo adored his new family. After the park, we'd sometimes go out for lunch, but one day I asked him back to my house and I made a Sunday lunch.

Oscar always slept after lunch, and I took him up to his bedroom. As I walked back down the stairs, Pablo was standing at the bottom. I tried to walk past him, but there was nowhere to go, and he reached for my hands. We stood looking into each other's eyes for a few seconds, then he leaned in and kissed me slowly on the lips. I opened my mouth and responded as he wrapped his arms around me and we kissed for what seemed like forever.

We walked back into the lounge holding hands and sat on the sofa, where we kissed again. I felt the tug of my heartstrings; he was almost perfect, took things easy and never put any pressure on me; he loved my son as much as he loved me. I dared to believe that God had sent this man to me to make my life complete.

He telephoned me the next day to tell me that he wanted to become a Christian like me. I was so happy; for once, my life was heading in the direction I wanted it to go.

The next couple of months were idyllic. In many respects, Pablo was the complete opposite of Lee, but it worked. Pablo had a steady job, regular income, something that was almost alien to me, and he insisted on paying for everything when we went out. He treated Oscar to ice creams and bought him toys, he couldn't do enough for us and our relationship blossomed, we were becoming closer and closer and I dared to believe that I had fallen completely in love with him, there was no doubt about it.

It was a Saturday evening and Lee appeared at the house looking quite serious. I invited him in.

"I want us to get back together and this time I'm serious."

"I'm dating someone else," I said. "You know that."

"Yes, but I'm serious, I'm ready to step up and I know what a complete bastard I've been to both you and Oscar."

It was a shock to my system.

"Really?" I said.

"Yes, I've never wanted anything more; I want to spend my whole life with you."

His words appeared genuine and yet at the same time sounded hollow to me. I told him how I was dating Pablo and how good he had been to Oscar.

"I know," he said. "I want to put that right. I've been selfish and I need to step up."

I'd heard it all before. Lee had let me down so many times. Each time before, my feelings for Lee lay under the surface; smouldering like ashes, ready to burst back into life. Somehow, this was different, and I reacted strangely to what he was saying. It was almost as if I'd erected a huge defence barrier between us and I wanted to test how serious he was about coming back into our lives.

I shook my head. "No, Lee, you had the chance when I proposed to you last leap year. I was serious about spending the rest of my life with you and you threw it back in my face."

"I know, I'm sorry."

"How sorry? I'm a Christian, Lee. I have to be married in the eyes of God before sleeping with any man. Nothing less will do for me and my son."

I could see how uncomfortable he was with the word marriage and I put him right on the spot, knowing exactly what his answer would be.

"So you're saying you are so serious about getting

back together? You want to marry me?"

"No," he said. "That's not what I said. I don't want to get married, but I—"

I nodded. "I thought not. You don't know what commitment or loyalty is, do you, Lee?"

He didn't reply. I asked him to leave and told him I was rebuilding my life. After he left, I stood behind the door, pressed my back against it and took a deep breath. In the old days, I would have been crushed by him leaving and the rejection but not now. I felt empowered; at last, I truly believed I had got Lee out of my system. As I walked through to the lounge, the phone rang. It was Pablo; he asked if he could accompany me to church in the morning.

"Of course you can," I said.

It was a beautiful service that day, and I could see that Pablo was fully integrated with the congregation and everything our church stood for. He'd even joined the men's football team. I was happier than anytime I could remember.

I don't need Lee, I said to myself.

After church, we were walking through the park. Oscar was running a little way ahead when Pablo took my hands and faced me. "I think we should get married."

"What?"

"I think we should get married," he repeated.

"But we've only been going out a few months."

"I don't care."

I could feel my heart pounding in my chest as I

struggled for words. "It's not much of a proposal, is it?"

He grinned. "It doesn't matter how I say it. I love you. I want to marry you and spend the rest of my life with you."

His words hit me like a sledgehammer. In less than twenty-four hours, two men had told me they wanted to spend the rest of their life with me.

I amazed myself at how cool I was with Pablo's proposal of marriage but it also dismayed and upset me that a man I'd been involved with was ready to move heaven and earth to be with me yet my son's father couldn't care less. They were polar opposites. I told Pablo I would think about it. It had come as a bit of a shock. He said he was fine with that; he'd wait for as long as I wanted.

Six months later, we were married. We'd only started dating for four months before Pablo proposed. Our church hosted the ceremony, where our friends, relations and close family shared the beautiful day with us. People had travelled from Portugal and Sweden just to be with us. The congregation also turned out in force; it seemed every person who had ever belonged to the church wanted to be there that day.

I couldn't have been happier and hummed the lyrics to the Luther Vandross song in my head.

My love, there's only you in my life
The only thing that's right

My first love, you're every breath that I take, you're every step I make.

Oscar was a page boy. I designed his outfit myself. A little black suit with a dog collar and a white shirt underneath. The jacket didn't do up in the middle like traditional suits. It had a diagonal slant with four silver buttons. I prided myself that I knew and thing or two about fashion.

My friend's son, Aaron, was the other page boy. They were both three years old and looked very handsome indeed.

I also designed the dresses for the two bridesmaids, baby-pink, silk dresses; each outfit was fitted perfectly and tailor-made. I had seen my dress in a magazine. It was fitted, with a ruche effect around the bodice and the waist. Simple but elegant.

Like a lamb to the slaughter, I thought, but I couldn't work out why.

This was my wedding day, the happiest day of my life, and everything about it was going to be original and perfect. I couldn't have been happier.

My future husband looked so handsome in his light grey Paul Smith designer suit and white shirt. None of our outfits were traditional and yet they perfectly encapsulated us; who we were and wanted to be. Modern, traditional but different, bespoke.

Oscar's godfather had a gold-coloured Rolls Royce, and he said he would be honoured to drive us to and from the wedding in his car. At last I had what

I always wanted. Real love.

We held the reception at Pablo's dad's place, where he worked as a chef. It accommodated almost two hundred people and we just about managed to fit all of our friends and family in. We thought a few of the guests invited from overseas may not have bothered to travel, but nobody said no, everyone wanted to be there.

We had also invited twenty-five of our special church friends, but as we enjoyed a glass of champagne, I looked around at the people mingling and to my absolute horror; I noticed more and more people at the reception who hadn't been invited.

I grabbed hold of Pablo. "Oh gosh, there's about a hundred people here who haven't been invited."

Pablo had noticed too, "They're all from the church; the entire congregation has turned up!"

I thought they would drift away as the invited guests started to take their place at the tables. But they didn't.

And yet it worked. I don't know how, but it worked out as those who didn't have a place setting congregated around the large bar. My father had put 'some money' behind the bar so there were no shortages of drinks. We had roast meats, and a whole dressed salmon, with every type of salad you could imagine accompanying it. Pablo's dad had pushed the boat out. It was a beautiful wedding lunch. As I looked over towards the bar, he had somehow conjured up more roast meats and three whole salmons; he armed the uninvited guests with knives and forks and tea plates; they all tucked in and nobody went hungry.

Even though I had an hour-long panic, we had a wonderful day. Pablo was so handsome and whispered in my ear towards the end of the night that he would look after me and Oscar forever. That was just what I wanted to hear. I craved a loving husband and father to my son. I drifted off to sleep that night, dreaming of our honeymoon and our long life together.

14

PAPERING OVER THE CRACKS

Within three months of our wedding, Pablo lost his job. My world didn't exactly come crashing down but it was as if some supreme being was toying with me and, just as my life rolled along on an even keel, it was as if someone was taking great pleasure in pulling the rug from under me as soon as I was getting comfortable.

For the first time in our relationship, we argued, mostly about money. Pablo had categorically stated that there were plenty jobs 'out there' for a man of his skill level but it proved more difficult than we both thought and, as the year drew to a close, he was still sitting around the house complaining about the various companies who hadn't even bothered to acknowledge his CV.

Money was tight, the house was bleak and as Christmas approached, we cancelled it. There was no rich food or parties, no family gathering or expensive presents for each other. We put a couple of hundred pounds to one side so that Oscar didn't go without presents and, although we had a nice family Christmas dinner with all the festive trimmings, we didn't even buy a bottle of champagne to toast our health or each other a gift.

Pablo got a new job in the new year; life improved, we bought our council flat and talked about children.

I didn't want to rush into pregnancy and, even though I had known Pablo as a friend and we had grown to love one another, I wanted us to have time to get used to living together. As Christians, there had been no sex before marriage.

We also needed a chance to bond properly as a family, and Oscar needed to get to know his new dad.

After our first wedding anniversary, we decided we would try for a baby. I fell pregnant almost immediately and our son, Lenny, was born in the summer. Like his older brother, he was walking at eight months. Nothing could hold our new family back now. We were on our way.

He proved to be as clever as his brother, a really fast learner. Five-year-old Oscar adored him and would play with him for hours. Lenny could talk quite early and, once he could string a few sentences together, the two brothers were inseparable.

But cracks appeared in the marriage.

Pablo's new job involved shift work. More often than not, he would work days, but then they threw more and more night shifts onto him and even insisted he worked the odd weekend. Pablo and I hated the unsociable hours.

I was working in the City. At first, things were fairly relaxed, so I could take Oscar to school and pick him up again. I worked in stockbroking and, in that industry, company take-overs were frequent and often. We had been taken over twice by this time, and I had another new boss. Although I worked part time, I was a conscientious worker and I would make sure I did my workload before I left the office every day. I was inputting data into the computer at a rate of knots that my colleagues couldn't believe, one or two of them even told me to slow down but I couldn't because I had to finish to pick the boys up and at least spend quality time with them before they went to bed. It caused major problems when it came to collecting the boys. Pablo and I couldn't get our hours right and we had to rely on the kindness of family and friends.

My new boss was putting pressure on me and didn't seem to understand that I was a part-time employee with two small boys. I longed for each week to end but it was getting more difficult as Pablo's boss called him in most Saturdays and the occasional Sunday too.

It soon dawned on me that my life was not much different from that of a single parent again. I looked after the kids, did the school run, ran off to work and sat at a computer for the rest of the day. It was like running on a hamster wheel and not getting anywhere.

I became conscious of a burning sensation in my left wrist during the middle of the week. By Friday, I was in constant pain. I convinced myself that it would go away over the weekend. It didn't help that Pablo was working again and all the chores had been left to me but the pain seemed to ease by Sunday afternoon.

I fired up my computer on Monday morning when I got back into the office and, as soon as I hit the first few keys on the keyboard, the pain was back with a vengeance. I tried to do my best but, in the end, I couldn't use my left hand at all. Luckily my boss was away for the day so I got on with my paperwork, stayed off the computer and made an appointment to see my GP.

The GP made me do a few exercises and referred me to a specialist consultant. He said he would sign me off work for two weeks. The pain subsided during the rest period but as soon as I got back to work, it came back within half an hour. I tried to get on with my work just using my right hand and then that hurt too. Eventually, I couldn't use either of my hands and the doctor signed me off work again, but this time for a month. I received the consultant's letter. They diagnosed me with Repetitive Strain Injury (RSI) commonly known as Work Related Upper Limb Disorder. The letter said that something had permanently damaged the nerve endings in my arms from, quote, 'working too intensely for continuous periods of time.' It devastated me.

I could do nothing with my hands. Everything hurt, even a simple task like holding a piece of paper. I called into the office to tell my colleagues I wouldn't be around for a while. Most of them wished me well but one or two of them thought I was faking it. They didn't believe I had RSI. There were a few wisecracks, but I didn't care about their opinion. My boss had the letter from the specialist and that was that.

They told me I needed complete rest, otherwise my condition would become permanent and that frightened the hell out of me. I couldn't do any housework, couldn't wash myself, hold a brush, drive, nothing for the first couple of months and, the worst thing was, I couldn't pick the boys up, hold them in my arms and hug them. All I could do was sit around. It was so depressing.

Pablo also started to have a go at me. On more than one occasion, he questioned why I couldn't wash the dishes or cook a meal that involved working with heavy pans. It wasn't what I wanted to hear, I needed support to get me through a very tough period of my life.

With RSI, there is nothing physical to see, no inflammation, no swelling or bruising. It's all internal and very, very painful. Unless you have experienced it, you have no idea what it feels like. I couldn't even make a cup of coffee without being in excruciating pain.

The GP arranged for me to have physiotherapy four times a week at first, and then gave me exercises to do at home. The treatment and the exercises helped a lot and eventually, the acute pain subsided. But I still couldn't carry anything heavy or do any work with my hands. After a year of going back to work then having to take time off again, they eventually made me redundant on medical grounds.

This didn't please Pablo as it meant a significant drop in monthly income. The doctor had also told me to forget about working for at least six months.

I had always worked; I had my first Saturday job at fifteen so not being able to work was very tough for me. I was determined not to let this situation keep me down and reasoned that I had to retrain in a role where using my hands was not essential. I immediately signed up for evening classes to train in management. After all I had run my own business before, I knew I could help other people to make a success of theirs.

I took the train to college, as driving was still not an option for me. Pablo had to take the role of parenthood very seriously, as there were things the doctor absolutely forbade me from doing. He had to take over most aspects of the housework and I could see from the outset that he was none too happy.

When the college gave me assignments, he refused to give me time to do the work and insisted I looked after the kids and put them to bed. My wrists and arms were okay at this point, but I knew it was madness to push it. Light housework, holding a pen and typing up the odd assignment, pushed my RSI to the limit, but he just couldn't see it. I had always been independent and so I could cope with this attitude, but all it did was drive us further and further apart.

We had already started marriage counselling with a lovely Christian couple. We were both in a meeting one evening when he accused me of faking RSI. He told the counsellors that I would do anything to get out of hard work.

This was tough to take. I felt let down and betrayed. I thought my husband knew me better than that. We had been married six years. I had never shirked a day's hard work in my life even when we sold up and moved to another house. Throughout our darkest financial hours, it had been me who had supported the family.

I knew my marriage was over; it was the last straw because I sincerely believed I had lost his trust and I had lost all respect for him. I was very disappointed in his behaviour towards me, but there was no grand plan for our future. I threw myself into my college work and my boys and got on with my life without his support around the house.

I passed my course with flying colours. It was an 'Access to University' course which was never my intention and I hadn't taken much notice of what opportunities my 'pass' would open up. My friend was doing the course so I had jumped on the bandwagon with her. It was as simple as that. Part of the course module was Law and I found it easy because it was the most interesting of all the classes and lectures. When we received our end-of-term marks, it was no surprise that Law was my highest mark. I was top of the class by a mile.

15

AN EXPENSIVE PAIR OF JEANS

The two detectives, DI Graham and his colleague, DI Holland, had a decision to make.

Whilst the armed robbery was at first thought to be an amateur job, the police had to admit that the gang had covered their tracks well. There were rumours that some of the robbers had even escaped on public transport and, although a few stolen items were beginning to resurface, there was nothing that would link anyone to the stolen goods; no physical evidence at least. It had been the footage on the CCTV from the jewellery store where their breakthrough had come and Holland was only too happy to take the credit.

One Friday night, the detectives left the pub in Soho much later than they had intended but made a promise that they would be at the station first thing Saturday morning. They wouldn't leave until they'd found something that could link Corey with the raid.

"A coffee, sir?" Holland asked.

"Too fucking right. It's a Saturday morning and I should be in bed. My head is banging away like Cozy Powell's drum... it needs caffeine."

Holland was too young to know who Cozy Powell was but figured from the comment that his boss wasn't feeling too good. He walked into the staff kitchen and clicked the kettle on. Three minutes later, he was back at the desk and was pleasantly surprised to see that Graham had already booted up the computer.

Holland placed the two coffees on the desk, then sat down. Graham located the CCTV file from Asprey Jewellers on the day of the raid. They both leaned forward as the film loaded and came into view. It was going to be a long day and they knew it.

The clock on the shop's recording read thirteen thirty-three when the first robber burst into the shop. Graham allowed the film to run at normal speed.

"We should study it frame by frame, sir," Holland said.

"Agreed, but we are only interested in the shooter, Corey. Wait till he comes in and then we'll slow it down."

The words had hardly left his lips when the robber with the shotgun burst through the door.

"Now," Graham said. He altered the speed and the

figure in the doorway froze like a statue. He altered it again to run on manual, one frame for every time he struck the enter key. They studied it until their eyes were stinging but rushed nothing; tracking the gunman's movements up to the point when he fired into the ceiling. He was close to the camera and they zoomed in on different points of his body, studying his clothing carefully.

"There!" Holland shouted. "Take it back a frame. The zip is down on his jacket and there's something there."

Graham took the camera back and immediately saw what Holland meant. "I see it, some sort of emblem on his jumper underneath."

"His hoody. Yes, sir, you can only just see it, but there's definitely some design or writing."

They took the footage back nine or ten frames and then forward another nine or ten to get the shot where most of the emblem had been revealed. Graham pressed enter and settled on one frame. He moved the cursor to the magnifying glass on the right-hand side of the screen and dragged it over to the middle of the gunman's chest. He zoomed in.

Holland leaned in further. "I think I recognise it, sir, it's specific letters of a US badge of a football or baseball team."

"Or basketball team, or college or university."

"Yes, one of those things."

They zoomed out. The four distinctive shapes formed the top part of the letters of the initials of a team. They were barely visible. Only half an inch of each letter could be seen, but the detectives knew they were tantalisingly close to something; a clue of sorts.

Graham chewed on a biro. "Anything like that in the clothes we took from Corey's gaff?"

"Can't think that there was, sir."

Holland was already on his feet and sitting at another computer. He logged in and located the file.

"Three hoodies and two sweats, all dark, either black or navy blue, but not any description of logos."

"Can you remember any logos or badges?"

"Can't say I do, sir. If you remember, we were more interested in getting all his dark clothing so we could get it to the lab."

Graham opened up Google search. He'd clicked on images and was keying in 'badges of American Football Teams'. He turned to Holland.

"You start on the basketball teams, major leagues and colleges and see if you can find anything that resembles those letters.

It was painstakingly laborious, old-fashioned police work, but it eventually paid off. They had been convinced that the top of the first letter had been a 'U' as there were two distinctive lines written in a fancy font which they later discovered was Comic Sans. The second letter was clearly a 'C', but they could find no football teams, baseball teams, basketball teams or ice hockey teams, beginning with UC.

It was Holland who eventually made the

138

breakthrough. "University of California and Los Angeles," he announced.

"You what?"

"UCLA. The University of California and Los Angeles," he repeated.

He had located a badge of UCLA in Comic Sans font and pressed print. The image slid out onto the printer tray five seconds later.

"There you go, sir. The shooter was wearing a UCLA hoodie. It's as plain as the nose on your face."

But there was a problem. Holland was fairly sure that none of the hoodies they'd recovered from Corey's flat were UCLA. Graham couldn't help but smile as he matched the letters up with the image on the computer screen. It was a little clue; no more than that.

Around four o'clock in the afternoon and, as far as Holland was concerned, the case was cracked wide open. They were about to pack it in for the day, more than a little satisfied that they had made progress on the hoodie.

Holland was still studying the footage. The gunman was running out of Asprey's. Graham had almost lost interest when a message from his wife came through on his phone

What time will you be home?

The clock on the recording of the CCTV read thirteen thirty-six. He located the zoom icon and centred the curser on the shooter's backside. He zoomed in.

139

"Well, I'll be fucked."

"What is it?" Graham asked.

Holland pointed to the screen. "There sir, on the arse of his jeans, a badge."

Sure enough, as Graham squinted at the screen and looked at the backside of the man with the shotgun running out of the shop, there was a small white patch on his back jeans pocket.

"Not just any old badge, Guv', Stone Island jeans."

"Who?"

"Stone Island, sir, designer wear, two hundred quid a pair."

"Two hundred quid!" Graham exclaimed. "What sort of lunatic pays that sort of money for jeans?"

"Exactly, Guv'. You walk into the street right now and pass a 1,000 people. You'd be lucky to see one of them wearing Stone Island jeans. They're as rare as rocking horse shit."

The cogs were turning in the senior detective's head.

Graham sank back into his seat. "Fuck me, this is big."

The young detective felt pleased with himself, but he was a little perturbed at the expression on Graham's face. It was a look of determination. Graham had a reputation in the force. A man who would always get the job finished.

"Get the fucker in here again." He pointed to the chair. "Get him in that fucking seat within the hour and get me the witness from the shop, the bird that

140

said he was handsome, built like a rugby player and at least six feet two tall. Let's work on her too. Let's make Corey sweat a little, and I want another warrant to search his gaff again."

Holland shook his head. "Are you sure, Guv?"

"Of course."

"But what if we don't find them?"

Graham took a few moments before he answered. "Don't mention the jeans to him. Say nothing; don't tell him what we are looking for. We'll find them, that's for sure, because nobody dumps a two hundred quid pair of jeans. They'll be there or they'll be at his bird's or his mother's or his brother's or someone that knows him and he'll eventually slip up."

Holland shrugged his shoulders. He wanted to tell his boss that there was a lot more work to do on this case. And yet Graham's hunches were legendary in the force and when convinced of a criminal's guilt, he was like a Rottweiler with a rabbit.

"You're sure he's the shooter?" Holland asked.

Graham nodded. "One hundred fucking percent and I'm a hundred and ten percent sure that we'll find exactly what we're looking for."

16

BRING HIM IN

They'd watched Corey from a distance for weeks. Despite their best efforts, they didn't catch him wearing a pair of Stone Island jeans. Graham was running out of patience. They raided Corey's apartment three days later and removed only one item, a pair of black Stone Island jeans. Despite searching high and low, they could not locate a UCLA sweatshirt. The detectives didn't seem too disappointed.

Two weeks later, Graham and his team were at City of London Magistrates' Court, Queen Victoria Street. Corey was there, too. They wanted him charged and remanded in custody. The evidence they presented was powerful.

It was Graham himself who delivered the nail in

the coffin. He read from his notebook as the magistrate looked on. He'd requested that a projector monitor be available in the Magistrates' Court that day and was pointing out the image from the CCTV footage, the image that showed the Stone Island, white belt buckle badge on the back of the jeans of the armed robber as he ran from the shop.

"The jeans are very expensive, sir. They retail at about two hundred pounds a pair so it's not just any old Tom, Dick or Harry we are dealing with here. Mr Corey has a reputation for designer clothing; he fits perfectly the description given by Ms Golightly from Asprey Jewellers, the unfortunate, young lady who was terrorised that particular day. We carried out a further raid on the accused's property exactly two weeks ago and removed a pair of Stone Island jeans, the same colour as the ones worn by the armed robber on the day of the raid on the jeweller's shop."

The chair magistrate, a District Judge, sighed. He was a stout elderly man with a rather unkempt beard and he'd seen it all before.

"DI Graham, I appreciate your enthusiasm, and I am aware of your long and distinguished service record. I have listened to what you have said today. However, I am not convinced that there is a real case to answer, nor do I think your one piece of circumstantial evidence warrants keeping Mr Corey behind bars."

It was exactly what Graham wanted to hear. The magistrate had played right into his hands. Graham pulled out the envelope and played his trump card. Graham spoke for only two minutes, then handed an envelope with Laboratory Test Results written on the front to the magistrate.

Lee stood in the dock and shook his head, muttering to himself, "No, this ain't right, this is a pack of lies."

He looked in desperation at his barrister, who didn't want to make eye contact. The magistrate remanded Lee Corey into custody. The case was going to trial.

17

HMP WANDSWORTH

Three months later.

HMP Wandsworth was a bleak place. Only eight miles from where Corey lived in Acton, it meant he had a steady flow of visitors; something to look forward to. It broke the monotony of time in prison. Being on remand was worse than being a normal prisoner because of the uncertainty. He almost envied some lads who knew they had a couple of years left to serve and could count the days off one by one.

Not Lee Corey. His days at the service of Her Majesty were in the lap of the gods, or rather in the hands of his barrister, John Buchanan, a middle-aged Scotsman, wise beyond his years. At least that's what he would tell anyone who was prepared to listen to him long enough. He spoke in a dull, monotone voice. It was enough to send you to sleep.

John Buchanan was Corey's only visitor one particular Friday at eleven in the morning. There was a knock on his cell door to tell him that his barrister had arrived.

"Get with it, Corey," the prison officer said. "Get your papers together and I'll take you down."

Bob Sinton was an old school type of screw, hard but fair with respect for certain types of prisoner. He'd seen it all in nearly thirty-five years of service. Nearing the end of his time, he just wanted to put in the last couple of years and get the hell out of there. Just like Lee.

Sinton whistled as he walked in front of the prisoners, cracking a few comments about the weekend's football and the shit weather he'd have to walk home in. He led him into the interview room where Buchanan and Lee exchanged pleasantries before they got down to business.

Buchanan opened his briefcase and took out a pile of papers. "The trial will be at the Old Bailey or one of the other central courts, such as Southwark or Blackfriars Crown Court. I should find out within the next month."

Why are you telling me this? Lee thought to himself, *What difference does the venue make?*

"You'll be allowed to wear your own clothes and you'll be kept in the court cells where you will be transported directly into the witness box. The witness box will be locked and have bulletproof glass to prevent anybody wanting to help you escape."

Lee let out a groan. "Fuck me, they're trying to make me look like Hannibal Lecter. That's gonna go down great with the jury."

Buchanan raised an eyebrow. "You're charged with armed robbery, I'm afraid, Lee, it's the norm. They can't take the chance that half a dozen of your armed robber mates might try to spring you."

Lee's head fell forward and he shook it from side to side. "Give me fucking strength."

The barrister continued, "The jury will be selected randomly from members of the public, normally six men and six women. They will have been asked if they have any link to you or the witnesses, or if they recognise any of the names. I've checked it out. It's fairly routine and the trial should start in about six months."

Corey fell back in his chair. "Six fucking months? You mean I'm in here for another six months?"

Buchanan left. He hadn't been there for more than twenty minutes. He seemed eager to get away.

Bob Sinton led Lee back to his cell. On the way, he told Bob what his barrister had said, mentioned that he would be inside for at least another six months.

"The system is fucked, son," Bob said. "Well and truly fucked."

18

A FORENSIC EXPERT

As expected, almost six months to the day, a jury was selected, sworn in and, in private, they chose a spokesperson, a stout, blonde lady in her fifties with a garish red jacket and a pale yellow blouse. Taking their places in the court, they were given instructions on what was expected of them.

"You must not, under any circumstances, discuss this case with anyone except a fellow juror." the clerk of the court said. "And you must not, under any circumstances, discuss the case at home with members of your family."

He told them about lunch and comfort breaks and said, in certain situations, they may take exhibits into the jury room once the court concluded the case. Thereafter, they could ask questions about the case while deliberating.

"Any questions you have will be heard in the presence of the barristers, the judge and the defendant. They will hear the questions and the answers given."

The clerk pointed out their pens and paper pads to make notes during the trial.

"You must not, under any circumstances, take your notes out of the jury room."

Corey listened intently as the clerk explained unanimous and majority decisions. He glanced towards Buchanan, who looked like he had heard it all before.

The spokesperson declared her jury had duly noted the conditions that they had to work under and the trial began with the prosecution and the defence opening statements.

Buchanan seemed in good, confident form, he claimed that there was no evidence or categorical CCTV footage to put his client in the location of the armed robbery that day and reminded the jury that it was up to the prosecution to prove beyond all reasonable doubt that his client had not only been there but had also been the man who had held the gun and pulled the trigger.

He wagged a finger at the jury, mimicking a school teacher telling off his pupils. "Beyond all reasonable doubt. Just remember that, ladies and gentlemen of the jury."

Corey was a worried man and he had good reason

to be. Some things had happened that were simply beyond his control. His brief hadn't been over positive, had held out little hope and said that the evidence of the jeans found in Corey's flat were, quote, 'a matter of grave concern.' Corey had been adamant the jeans weren't his. His brief had advised him to change his plea to guilty... it wasn't too late, he'd said the judge would look favourably on the fact he didn't want to waste any more of their time.

"The jeans aren't mine," he repeated to his barrister during a recess period.

Buchanan looked towards the ceiling, then glanced at his watch. "C'mon, we'd better get back in there."

Corey dared to take a slight glance at the jury; he wiped a bead of sweat from his top lip as he sat in the bulletproof witness box. He was frightened, more frightened than he had been at any stage of his life. He looked to his left towards the public gallery.

She was there. Of course she was there. She would always be there. He caught his breath; his mouth was dry. It should have been all so different. Why wasn't she his wife? Why weren't they living together... as a family, a big happy family? Why hadn't he committed to her and their son? Why and how had he fucked up so badly? He stared at the two detectives who had led the investigation; DI Graham and DI Holland.

"That's why," he whispered under his breath. "They've stitched me up, that's why."

The trial lasted five days. The prosecution had

worked out their strategy to perfection considering the lack of evidence. It was like a well-orchestrated plan, a movie where the cinema-goer is fed just enough information to cast doubt in their minds. It was a who dunnit, a John Grisham court drama book where the final few pages would bring the perpetrator to justice and the reader would be left in no doubt as to his guilt. Lee could feel the case slipping away.

At first, the prosecution appeared to have built their case around the tip-off and the girl in Asprey Jewellers. She had described the man with the shotgun. She had described Lee Corey almost perfectly. The only thing that was missing was a facial description.

Lee gazed across at the jury and tried to figure out which way they were leaning, simply by the look on their faces.

There were ten white jurors and that concerned him. He'd never played the race card in his life, didn't need to. Being big and black in his line of work paid dividends. No one fucked with him. He made sure of that. It was true England, had more than its fair share of bigots and racists but this was London, his territory where 40% of the population came from all corners of the world, here amongst the people, most didn't give a shit about the colour of someone's skin. His mates were white, black, Asian. It didn't matter one iota and, on the whole, the capital worked well in a multi-cultural mix of nearly nine million individuals. Lee had no issues walking the streets, frequenting his favourite pubs or dining out. His money was the same colour as anybody else's and he loved London.

He didn't like juror number four though, an elderly white man in his late sixties or the smarmy-looking woman at the end. He worried.

Those jeans, those fucking jeans.

* * *

Of course, I was going to go to the bloody trial. It was the curiosity factor; I had to know if the stupid bastard was guilty or if he was just a stupid bastard that had been set up. I couldn't believe it when Shirley told me he had been nicked for armed robbery. I wanted to see for myself. Every day since the trial started, I had been there; now it was day five, the day that both sides presented their final arguments and their closing speeches. I somehow sensed that the prosecution was about to play their trump card.

The prosecution barrister, Hubert Watson, stood. "Your Honour, I'd like to bring in a forensic specialist."

The judge nodded in approval and a smartly dressed man in his mid-forties walked to the witness box and took his place. He was sworn in. I didn't like his demeanour. He was cocky looking, too full of himself.

Peter Tremlett introduced himself as a forensic specialist who operated out of an independent laboratory in Birmingham. He produced a clear, sealed bag with a pair of Stone Island jeans inside, exactly the type that Lee loved to wear and, at that, I was sure the trial was over.

The prosecution claimed they had found the jeans in Lee's flat during a second police search. Lee's barrister said his client had never seen the jeans before and yet the forensic specialist confirmed that not only was Lee's DNA on the jeans but also traces of gunshot residue. The final nail. That's what had been in the envelope Graham handed to the magistrate when he remanded Lee into custody.

Buchanan got to his feet. His argument was weak as he tried to tie the forensic scientist in knots without success. But Tremlett was calm, said that the gunshot residue had been found on the front right-hand side of the jeans which tied in with the CCTV footage of the gunman firing the shotgun with his right finger on the trigger, the butt of the weapon tucked into his right shoulder while holding the stock with the palm of his left hand.

I watched as the jury looked on and the play unfolded. That's what it was, a big bloody charade, a game where the best barrister wins. Even I was leaning towards a guilty verdict, despite my conflict of interest in that I had once loved the defendant with all of my heart. It wasn't looking good for him at all. Tremlett confirmed that although someone had washed the jeans clean, the lab had found a pubic hair in the zip. It was an exact match to Lee's DNA.

It was the prosecution barrister's turn on his feet.

He looked over towards the forensic scientist and said, "I have no further questions."

There was a collective gasp around the courtroom and the tension was palpable; it was a good play by the barrister. By asking nothing more, he confirmed that what the scientist had said could not be disputed. It was gospel, as simple as that. They were Lee's jeans.

He turned to the judge and asked permission to play the CCTV footage from the day of the robbery. The judge consented and I watched as a granular black-and-white image appeared on a large projector screen at the far side of the courtroom.

The barrister took the remote control in his right hand and fast-forwarded the footage to where the armed robber entered the shop.

"I want you, ladies and gentlemen of the jury, to observe as I take you through what must have been quite a horrendous experience for the poor souls who were working in the shop that day. Look at the terror on their faces, the fright when he discharges the weapon."

He slowed the footage down and zoomed in on the gunman as he fired into the ceiling. A second or two later, a ghostly cloud of plaster dust floated eerily to the floor.

"You have heard the evidence from our forensic scientist, Mr Tremlett, an expert whose lab has confirmed not only that the defendant's DNA was on those jeans, but that they also held traces of gunshot residue." He paused for dramatic effect and looked across to where Lee sat in the witness box. "And the defendant says he has never seen those jeans before."

The barrister smiled; a sickening smile. I wanted to slap him. And yet he wasn't finished.

He spoke to the court clerk who walked over to where the jeans were lying and removed them from the polythene bag. He walked over to the jury and handed the jeans to the spokesperson.

"Stone Island jeans," he said. "Very expensive designer wear, way out of reach of the working man. Feel the quality, madam, and please, hand them down the line, let your jurors examine them by all means."

He waited and watched as the jurors handed the jeans from one member to the next.

"Take special note of the white patch on the back, a patch that will prove very important within the next few minutes."

He held up the remote control again and moved the CCTV footage forward frame by frame. It showed the gunman turning and running towards the door. The barrister slowed the footage down; each frame took more than a second. He stopped the footage as the gunman neared the door and zoomed in further, steering the magnifying glass image onto the back of the jeans. I knew exactly what was coming and sure enough, the white patch from the Stone Island jeans appeared in the middle of the screen. The Stone Island writing on the bottom of the patch was barely visible, but my heart sank. He was guilty. How could he have been so stupid as to wear those jeans and then leave them in his flat?

I couldn't help myself. I stared over at Lee. He looked like a little boy lost as he shook his head from side to side. The prosecution barrister was all but finished as the jeans were collected from one of the jury members.

"These jeans are rare, ladies and gentlemen of the jury," he said. "They retail at over two hundred pounds a pair."

One or two of the jury looked genuinely surprised.

He continued. "I put it to you that the jeans you have just inspected, the Stone Island jeans with the defendant's DNA on were the same jeans worn by the gunman in Asprey Jewellers on that same Saturday when the staff of that store were put in fear of their lives, traumatised beyond belief."

Lee sat in the witness box, shaking his head as the barrister continued.

"These jeans are Mr Corey's, ladies and gentlemen. These jeans were worn by the gunman I have just pointed out on the CCTV footage; they are the exact same jeans. The gunman and Mr Corey are one and the same person."

Lee lost it. He couldn't prevent himself and leapt to his feet. "They aren't my jeans," he screamed at the barrister as he banged on the bulletproof glass.

Buchanan jumped up and urged him to sit down. There followed a minute or two of pandemonium as a policeman and a security guard appeared on the scene and the judge called for order in his court. Eventually, Lee regained his composure.

I watched as Buchanan made his closing statement but, I confess, hardly a single word sank in. It was a very poor performance and focused on the one circumstantial piece of evidence, the jeans that the police had claimed to have found in Lee's flat. It was almost as if Buchanan was doing the prosecution's job for them and, just before he sat down, he reminded the jury yet again that they could only convict the defendant if it was beyond all reasonable doubt that he was the armed robber in the shop who had fired the shotgun into the ceiling. It may have only been circumstantial evidence, but from where I was sitting, it was bloody convincing. The judge ordered the jury to retire and the police led Lee away. The first of my tears fell and I reached into my bag for a tissue.

It was two days later when I received a phone call from Lee's sister to say that the jury had arrived at a decision and were sitting later that day. I got to the court with twenty minutes to spare. I was trembling as they led Lee back into court in handcuffs. They moved him towards the door of the glass cage, removed the cuffs and eased him in before locking the glass door.

He glanced over at me. We made eye contact and I saw a flicker of a smile. It quickly disappeared.

"Ladies and gentlemen of the jury, have you arrived at a decision?"

The spokesperson stood. "We have, Your Honour."

She said that they had agreed on a majority decision and asked the judge if he would accept it. Ten of the jurors had agreed on the same decision. The other two hadn't been able to decide either way; in effect, they had abstained in the vote. The judge said that he would accept the verdict of ten jurors.

"And do you find the defendant, Lee Corey, guilty or not guilty of armed robbery?"

"Guilty, Your Honour."

* * *

On the day of Lee's sentencing, I couldn't remember how I got to cafe Nero on Newgate Street. I have no recollection of the walk there, ordering a strong Americano coffee or carrying it over to a single seat by the window. I sat at the long bar, gazing out into the throngs of London shoppers and workers as they went about their daily business.

I watched a girl in a red coat carrying a large shopping bag wishing that I could somehow miraculously swap places with her. Her life was surely better than mine. Lee had been sentenced to fifteen years and, when it was read out, my world came crashing down; I realised how much I still loved him.

I can only describe that moment as close to bereavement. I was in a dark place with a wreck of a marriage to Pablo. Although we were still living in the same house, with him working nights, I knew my marriage was all but over and I was living as a single mum with two boys and I had a recognised disability.

I sat for over two hours, had another three strong coffees, and almost floated out of the place. I telephoned my childminder and, for a ridiculous fee, she agreed to keep the boys for the night. She had made plans, she told me; it was Friday night. I sent a message out to a couple of my good friends and we met up in one of my favourite bars in Soho. I needed support and alcohol as I had never needed it before.

19

A PARTING OF THE WAYS AND A NEW LIFE

At thirty-five, I was delighted to be accepted into Kingston University after my Access course; it was a proud moment for me. The local authority, after assessing my disability, gave me a computer with a voice-activated package. I was flying; nothing could stop me now as I threw myself into it and tried to erase Lee and his life of crime from my memory.

During my assessment, they discovered I had dyslexia, which surprised me because I had no genuine problems in that area. However, it came with extra funding and with that support; I dared to dream that leaving university with a Law degree was a real possibility.

There was a lot of work to do. I remember my first

Friday when the lecturer gave us 100 pages to read by Monday morning on top of the written assessments and research. I was shocked and that was only one subject! It was tough. I was a mature student with two children to look after without any help from my husband. He was a husband in name only; there was absolutely nothing between us anymore despite us living in separate bedrooms under the same roof.

I watched the younger students who didn't have a care in the world and at times felt sorry for myself. But those thoughts didn't last long, and I knuckled down with a determination that surprised me.

By the end of year two of university, my divorce with Pablo was almost completed and the stress I was under was unbelievable. But I kept going. I told myself it was either this or the dole and I would never be on the dole. Six months later, he moved out and I felt a huge load lift from my mind. The energy I had been using up arguing and trying to make things bearable between my husband and I could now be directed to my studies. The divorce was straightforward. We agreed to split the assets.

During this time, Oscar got into the school of my dreams, one of the best schools in the country, a co-ed fee-paying private school and, despite me having no regular income, nothing was going to stop him from going. It was a school I discovered when I was pregnant with him. I had waited eleven years. He won a place after competing against 400 children for 50 places. I was very proud of him. When the letter arrived; it was the day before his birthday. We had applied for other schools, but this one was top of my list. I cried tears of joy until he got home and then I handed him the letter.

As he read it and the news sunk in, I blurted out, "Congratulations." I gave him a big hug and kiss.

Nothing more needed to be said.

But Pablo had been speaking with my father and they felt they needed to sit down and give me a reality check. They said Oscar couldn't go to the school because we couldn't afford it. My faith in God was resolute. I looked at both of them and said, "Don't even worry about it. God is in control and He will take care of it."

And He did. Within a few weeks of receiving the letter from the school, I won the case against my former employers relating to the RSI injury I developed; they discriminated against me on racial and disability grounds and I settled out of court. With the redundancy money and a pay-out, I had enough money for eleven-year-old Oscar's first year of school fees. I also bought a second-hand convertible car, something I had always wanted.

I topped up my income by offering home tuition to foreign students who wanted to learn English and the money I earned from that went directly to pay Oscar's school fees. This was a lot to manage and the studies were draining me because I put my heart and soul into them; something or someone was telling me that these were important for the future.

I'd see to my students during the day, squeezing in an hour or two of uni study when I could and then play mummy again when the kids came in from school. It was ten o'clock at night before the dishes and other chores were finished, then I would sit down and study until one or two in the morning. At six in the morning, I was up again, a little more study and then the school run. Studying Law was tough, I knew that but I was determined to throw everything I could at it. It was time-consuming, a subject that couldn't be skipped over or blagged. Some students studying other subjects laughed and bragged about how little effort they put into their course but with Law that wasn't possible, it required countless hours reading course materials, notes and books. There was a lot of concentration needed to absorb everything before I even started to write my assignments. And yet I loved it; even on the mornings when I crawled into bed exhausted knowing that I had to get up again in a few hours. I wouldn't have swapped it for the world.

Of all the degrees one could opt to study, Law was one of the hardest. There was not a single day off, apart from Christmas Day and Easter Sunday. The rest of the time was taken up reading coursework, researching, writing assignments and preparing for exams. At the weekends, my step-mum came to my rescue and babysat. When friends and family were out partying and socialising, I went to the library. The only people there were Law students. Bar school was not much better, forensic accounting, tax, advocacy, knowing your client, vulnerable witnesses we covered it all... nothing was left to chance. There were exams at each stage, performance was videotaped and replayed, with 'constructive criticism', there was no downtime, no getting used to the change in pace. Everyone was expected to learn fast and to raise their game even faster.

Law is not a profession for the faint-hearted, as they say, learn it or die trying. The pressure was always on, a pass mark was never enough. The three year Law course needed far higher marks than just the standard pass mark to obtain a degree. After that, there was a year for the bar course. More pressure. The next stage was a year of pupillage. Even higher expectations than before. A pupillage is a period of practical training required to become a fully-fledged barrister so I needed to work almost full-time under the wings of experienced barristers. How the hell was I going to fit that in? But I had to do it, I would have to develop vocational skills and understand the exact practice areas perfectly. As I read through the book I had picked up from the library, I studied a paragraph that made my heart sink. Only thirty-seven percent of eligible pupillage candidates got through and candidates could only apply once a year to a maximum of twelve chambers. If you didn't get a pupillage you would have to wait for another twelve months before applying again.

My first attempt at getting pupillage came to nothing. I got two interviews and felt quite proud of myself. Although I felt that the interviews had gone well, it was a case of thanks but no thanks. I couldn't quite understand why I hadn't been accepted and now I had to wait another twelve bloody months before I applied again. I polished up my application and also the separate letter of why I had chosen that particular chamber.

I wrote what I believed the chambers wanted to see; hardworking, fully committed to justice, my lifelong ambition, that kind of stuff. Before sending it off for the second time, I asked some barristers I had been shadowing for advice. I wanted their opinions. By then I realised that two interviews out of a twelve was not a good return. One barrister, Garry, gave me some good advice.

He looked at a copy of my letter and said, "I can't see you in here."

"What do you mean?"

"Well, there is nothing about who you are, the fact that you are a mature student, what made you come to the bar, what struggles and sacrifices you had to go through."

"Yes," I protested, "but surely they don't want to read about that?"

"Yes, they do. That's what makes you stand out, and your struggles are exactly what they want to read about. It's what makes the difference. You haven't given up, even though it would have been so easy to do just that. You have overcome multiple obstacles and challenges just to get here. It is precisely what they want to see."

But although I had an entire year before I could submit again, I rewrote my covering letter and a week later sent it over for him to have a look. He approved. Only twelve months to wait. I beefed up my application by taking a Master's degree at King's College London in Criminology and Criminal Justice. I wanted to know what causes someone to commit a crime and I volunteered one day a week at the Prisoner's Advice Service, giving legal advice to prisoners about their rights.

It was perfect. By the time I submitted my application again the following year, I had a merit for my Masters from Kings and an entire year of advising prisoners. I elected to apply to Human Rights Chambers, who hopefully would understand my mind-set. It worked, I got an interview. I still wasn't over the line, though; each chamber receives about 1,000 applications for each pupil position. The Pupillage Committee must choose 100 applicants and out of those, they select fifty for an in-depth examination, twenty of them are selected for interview. I was one of three students chosen for the Chambers of Lord Griffiths QC, a vigorous advocate for justice and equality in his personal and professional life. I was ecstatic.

20

HMP LONG LARTIN

Lee had been in prison for a while when I went to university. It was hard trying to keep up with the enormous amount of work needed to pass the exams. Luckily, there was a decent-sized group of mature students and we helped and supported each other. Some of us had not studied for around twenty years, so it was a culture shock. Some students dropped out after year one, but I had been determined *not* to be one of those.

One student reminded me that year one at university does not go towards your final mark, so all I needed to do was to pass. That was a relief because it took most of that first year to get into the flow of study, family, and sleep. There was a lot of strain on me, but nothing was going to stop me from achieving my goal.

Oscar knew his father was in prison from when he was, six years old, but thankfully he was too young to know what prison was, what his father had done, and how long he was going to be locked up for. I seldom discussed Lee with Oscar except when we agreed Lee's sister would take him to visit his dad. Visits were on Lee and Oscar's birthday and at Christmas or on special occasions. I wouldn't send him any more than that. I gave him warning of what to expect when I'd casually drop into the conversation that he'd be going to see daddy next Saturday.

He'd be excited, of course, and I tried to make it a bit of a special treat, allowing him sweets and fizzy drinks. I hated fizzy drinks, but twice a year was okay. When his aunt brought him back, I would allow him a takeaway. I didn't want to see Lee, but I wanted our son to maintain some semblance of contact with him and thankfully she'd agreed. It was an enormous weight off my mind.

I knew he would cope. He was young enough and he was blinkered by the fact that he would be seeing his dad. So it had worked.

It was the day before Lee's birthday in January and as usual Oscar was excited. I'd bought him a card and a small present to give to his dad. The day before he was due to be collected a call came from his aunt.

"You're not going to believe this, Cookie," she said. "I'm so sorry, but my car has broken down. They've towed it to the garage and they want the best part of five hundred pounds to fix it."

She said she didn't have the money to get it repaired for at least a few weeks and subsequently she was unable to take Oscar to see his dad. I said I understood and gazed over to where he stood by the door, still smiling and yet listening intently to the conversation. He sensed there had been a major development.

"Am I still going to see Dad?" he asked.

I looked over at him. How could I say no?

We caught the train from King's Cross station at nine the following morning. It was too stressful for me to drive. It was the weekend, so thankfully the train was half empty. The journey took three hours and Oscar and I played cards looking out the window occasionally as the train wound its way through the pretty Chiltern Hills, into Oxfordshire and eventually into the Cotswolds. It was such a different environment from London, so green and peaceful and I had to remind myself that something grim would be waiting for us at the journey's end.

The station nearest to the prison was Honeybourne, ten miles away in the middle of nowhere, and we got a taxi from the station to the prison. I took a deep breath as we arrived. It wasn't what I expected. HMP Long Lartin wasn't the enormous fortress, castle-like prison I had anticipated. It looked like a 1970s office complex. I hated it from the outset.

As soon as we got there, they took my fingerprints

and checked our ID. They told us to take a seat in a waiting area; we sat around and waited to be called in. It was soul-destroying in the waiting room with other families wanting to see their loved ones. The environment made me feel like a criminal and there were a lot of unfortunate people in there. I don't think I had seen so many tattoos in my life, and everybody was smoking, even a young teenager was having a puff while his mother looked on as if it was the most natural thing in the world.

The authorities had tried their best to make the place as friendly as possible but it didn't work. There was a canteen run by volunteers so that helped a little but I couldn't help feeling as though I had done something wrong… just by association. The prison staff were very matter of fact, everyone had to take off their shoes and be subjected to a body search. All personal effects had to be left in a locker and then you were handed the locker key; your £10 in small change was checked by a prison officer to make sure you weren't taking in a penny more. The whole process from arrival at the prison complex to going through security took the best part of an hour.

We eventually walked into the visitors' area. There were plastic tables and chairs bolted to the floor, three chairs per table, and in the corner was a play area for the kids. Oscar had been there before and was pretty unphased by it all but for me the atmosphere was oppressive, dark and depressing.

All I could hear was the jangle of keys, locks being

opened and doors slamming shut. Eventually, the prisoners were led into the room, one by one. When we arrived in the main room, there was CCTV everywhere and a large desk where two prison officers sat with a list of visitors' names in front of them. One of them looked up.

"I'm here to see Lee Corey," I said sheepishly.

I was only there for Oscar, and neither one of us belonged in a place like this. What was this institution and how could Lee end up here? My heart was racing as they directed me not to a plastic table with secure chairs but to another area altogether. We walked over to the far side of the visitors' area, to some cubicles. There were three or four of them, partitioned off from the main room with huge glass screens.

I turned to the prison officer who hovered in the doorway. "What's this?" I asked.

"It's a closed visit, madam. There is no contact allowed between the prisoner and his family."

"But why?"

"You'd better ask him that," he replied.

And then he was gone, closing the door behind him.

The walls were glass. There were two plastic chairs, so I sat down and tried to shuffle my chair a little forward. There was no movement. These too, were bolted down. While I waited for Lee, I could see other prison officers monitoring me.

It seemed like an age before he appeared. I heard more keys, and then the door swung open and locked immediately. Lee walked in and stood at the other side of the glass. He hunched his shoulders and held his head down as he trudged to the cubicle where we sat.

I turned to Oscar and smiled. "Here's your dad," I said, and he smiled back at me.

I reminded myself this trip was all about Lee's son. It meant nothing to me. I wanted to ensure that Oscar's needs were met... as far as I could manage. Lee was his father, after all, and no matter what he had done, we could never change that fact. Lee sat down and smiled at Oscar; I sat back and took it all in.

His voice went up an octave and he tried to sound jolly for his son, but I could see through the tears that were welling up in my eyes that it was all a big act. I squirmed in my chair. This wasn't supposed to happen. I'm not supposed to feel like this and I certainly did not want to cry, not in front of my son and not in front of Lee, but I couldn't stop myself. He looked like a caged animal.

"What have you done?" I whispered through the tears.

Lee looked at me. I felt my heart rip in two. "I'm sorry," he said.

"Why?" I asked.

He said nothing.

"How in hell has it come to this?"

Silence. I thought I detected a slight shrug of his shoulders, but couldn't be sure. I reached in my pocket for a handkerchief and pretended to blow my nose as I wiped at the tears that were streaming down my face. I hoped Oscar didn't notice, he was fixated on his father.

I reminded myself that this was Oscar's visit. It was nothing to do with me; this was for him. The conversation turned to what he had got for Christmas, his favourite Gameboy games and what he'd been up to. Oscar was playing hockey for the school team and had started basketball. Lee was genuinely excited. He had been a natural at basketball and, when he was a teenager, he got an offer to go to the United States to play.

He told Oscar, "I could have gone to America to play professionally, but I turned it down."

There was a smile on his face.

Idiot, I thought.

I still felt angry every time I thought about it. Why did he turn down the opportunity of a lifetime? He could have made something of his life; he could have left this pile of shit life behind, the life he had already created for himself where the police visited his parent's house nearly every day. Who does that?

Fucking imbecile, went through my head.

An hour and a half passed quickly and yet every second dragged by too, if that makes any sense. Before we knew it, the prison guards were shouting in the main room that there were only a few minutes of visiting left. I hated the place, the military feel to it, the discipline, the clock and being made to feel that you should be behind bars too. I couldn't wait to get my son out of there. Everything about the visit was dreadful and leaving was no better. There was so much to say, so much to ask about how he was doing, if it was okay. And yet I had asked him nothing before it was time to go. I got a question out about the closed visit when the other prisoners were in the main hall and he mumbled something about a fight with another prisoner. I couldn't understand what he was alluding to, but this was his punishment, one that meant his son suffered the most.

As we stood up, a prison officer told us that all visits would be 'closed' for the next few months. I hated every inch of the glass-encased cubicle and yet I didn't want to leave.

I tried to look upbeat, to smile and be cheerful for Oscar, but it was hard.

We had a long journey back to London. I felt emotionally and phyisically drained. We had some food and little treats for the journey home, so, at least for Oscar, it was not too bad. He didn't say much, he was quiet, he internalised his thoughts and feelings or perhaps he even kept quiet for my sake. He might have sensed how hard it was for me. He was an intuitive child.

I knew it wouldn't be long before Oscar needed to be back again and I was determined that the responsibility for taking him was firmly back onto Lee's sister. Her car was being fixed now. This time, there were no excuses. Wild horses wouldn't drag me back to Long Lartin as long as I lived. It was a long way; it was expensive; I had better things to do with my time and my money. And realistically, how the hell was I going to fit in prison visits with everything I had on my plate?

When we got home at about seven that evening, the phone rang. It was Lee. He said it had been lovely to see me and thanked me for coming and for bringing Oscar.

Then I opened my mouth. "I can come and see you again if you want?"

"That would be nice," he said.

Did I just say that? I wondered.

Yes, I had. I couldn't help myself. When Lee had looked at me in that closed visit cubicle, something had stirred in my heart and, as much as I wanted to fight it, I knew I was still in love with him. Nothing had changed.

21

"THEY WEREN'T MINE COOKIE."

When I awoke the next morning in the cold light of day, I cursed myself for being so stupid. I cursed myself for saying I would go to see him again. Every single part of me was shouting, "No!" It was stupid, simply not practical; I would leave it to his family. I convinced myself it was their responsibility.

The next day, Lee called me on the phone. I tried to distance myself from him and luckily Oscar was there, so I passed him on to his dad. He had a big smile plastered across his face, and his reaction made me melt. I had to remind myself that this was not the first time for him, as it was for me. I marvelled at my son's resiliance, although I would not put him through that nightmare too often.

Yet, as I watched Oscar talk to his father, I realised

it hadn't been such an ordeal for him. He had taken it all in his stride. I had played it down and controlled it, which helped. We had played games on the train and I answered his questions about the visit without making it into a bigger drama than it was.

I listened as he talked on the phone to his dad for at least ten minutes. There was no shortage of conversation and in that time, I made my mind up that taking Oscar to see his dad didn't need to be a problem. I could fit the time in and, even though it was going to be expensive, I knew I could handle it right. I wouldn't let my son down the way Lee's family had.

It disappointed me that we, including Oscar, didn't interest them, either before or after Lee went to prison. They didn't care how we were coping. Each year from when Oscar was born, I had invited them to his birthday parties, but they never came. There wasn't even a card or a present. Occasionally, they turned up to see us if there was something in it for them. When his mum moved to Jamaica, we visited her and brought back gifts. The family were right in there for the spoils. That they never visited Lee in prison except his sister who occasionally took Oscar, didn't surprise me.

I decided that after the hassle of his aunt's car breaking down and who was going to take Oscar to see his father the first time; it was best if I did it. My son needed structure and stability. I could give him that. A couple of weeks later, I took another phone call from Lee and we arranged our next visit. Thirty-six hours later, I was back in Long Lartin prison with Oscar.

Another bloody closed visit.

For fuck's sake! My mind reeled.

If I had expected the second visit to be easier than the first, then I had been kidding myself. I didn't belong in a place like this, neither did my son. Looking at Lee, I felt sick. Something told me he didn't belong there either. He asked me how I was.

"Fine," I said.

Our eyes met and, at that moment, the resistance, the anger, the denial melted away... again. He had a habit of doing this to me. His eyes dismantled the barriers I had put up and the walls I had built. Once again the tears rolled down my face. I couldn't take it. Something was screaming at me. He didn't belong in prison. He wasn't meant to be there.

Oscar was trying to console me, asking what was wrong. He couldn't take it in, of course, because his dad and I hadn't lived under the same roof for most of his life, he didn't make the connection that Lee's incarceration was too much for me to cope with. After all when we split up he was just a toddler and he'd never had his dad at home with him as part of the family. In fact seeing him in prison was the most stable contact Oscar had had with him. After ten minutes, Oscar asked me if I wanted anything as he got up to go off to the visitors shop for some drinks and snacks for us to have. The visitors' shop was a makeshift stall set up in the visitors hall, run by little old ladies, normally from a local church, volunteers, who tried their best to make the visits as humane as possible in that God forsaken place. They served tea, coffee, biscuits, sweets, crisps and cold drinks at cost price. As usual there was a long queue.

As he walked away, I started crying again.

"Don't cry," Lee said softly and went as if to touch my cheek, which he couldn't because three inches of bulletproof glass divided us.

And then anger.

"How could you do this?" I sobbed. "Why would you do this to yourself? Why would you risk your freedom, the chance to see your son grow up?"

I will never forget that moment as long as I live. He shrugged his shoulders and raised an eyebrow.

"I didn't," he said. "It wasn't me. They fitted me up."

I couldn't help myself. "Are you fucking kidding me?"

"I was fitted up," he repeated. "Those jeans were planted."

"The jeans? What do you mean, the fucking jeans?"

"The Stone Island jeans. They weren't mine."

I thought back to the trial. The evidence appeared overwhelming; the jeans found in Lee's flat, the CCTV footage, the DNA and the gunshot residue. For fuck's sake, everyone in that court thought he was guilty.

It was a slow-motion moment. I looked over towards Oscar who has moved a few places nearer the front of the queue, the volunteers did their best but they weren't the fastest servers in the world!

I looked back at Lee. He was talking to me through the speaker in the glass, his head slightly bowed. Saying something about the jeans. The words didn't register. I looked over at Oscar again and he looked up and shrugged. I guessed he was used to the slow pace. He waved and I waved back. He'd been excited to see his dad again although he didn't ask me details. By now, he had a rough idea of why his dad was in there, although I never told him. I swore our son would never end up in a place like this, full of villains and criminals, rapists, thieves, murderers and of course, armed robbers. I had made sure his home life couldn't have been more different.

Lee's words snapped me out of my daydream.

"I would never wear fake shit, you know that."

"What?"

"The jeans, Cookie, the Stone Island jeans. They were fake. They weren't mine."

I didn't want to hear his lies. I pointed at Oscar. "Your son," I said. "Were you thinking about him when you walked into that jeweller's shop?"

"You're not listening to me, are you?"

"Oh, I'm listening alright; I'm listening to a criminal talking bullshit. For fuck's sake, Lee, I watched that CCTV footage too. The robber looked like you. He even moved like you."

Lee shook his head, looked as if he was going to speak, but dropped his head.

My mind flashed back to one of my favourite movies, the Shawshank Redemption. Andy and Red, Morgan Freeman's character, had just met. Andy protested his innocence. Freeman smiles. He throws a softball as he looks back at Andy.

"Everybody in here is innocent, didn't you know that?" he said. He calls to the prisoner who catches his softball, "Hey, what are you in for?"

The prisoner replies, "Didn't do it, lawyer fucked me over."

I looked up. "Your lawyer fucked you over. Is that it Lee?"

He eased back in his seat as he spoke. His voice was weaker, more distant away from the small speaker.

"Not Buchanan, the Old Bill, Cookie. It was the Old Bill that fucked me up."

Never had I experienced so many emotions in such a short time.

Why did he do this to me? I'd loved him when I walked into the visitor's area. Then there was the embarrassment and the feeling of not belonging, the shame and guilt, guilty by association; the fact I was even there made me one of them, one of the criminal set. But I didn't care, I'd accept that. But now... the anger... the rage, the sheer frustration that my son's father had confined himself to more years inside than his son had been on the planet and, what was worse, he was lying to me. That's what hurt me the most because by the time he got out of prison, his son would be a young man tinkering with cars and messing about with girls.

"You're fucking ridiculous. Do you know that?" I said as I stood up.

"Where are you going?"

"I'm leaving."

I shouted over to Oscar. "C'mon Oscar, we are going."

"Please no, don't go, there's still an hour to go."

I ignored him as Oscar approached me with the cold drinks and crisps in his hand.

"We'll eat that on the way back," I said to him. "We have to go, sorry. Say good bye to your dad!"

I turned my back on Lee. "The jeans, Cookie," he repeated. "They weren't mine, babe."

The prison officers looked a little confused and yet they must be used to disagreements between prisoners and visitors; violent outbursts of frustration. As we walked away, I could still hear Lee pleading with me. He was lying to me again. He had to be.

22

WE ALL MAKE MISTAKES

It was three in the morning when I looked at the clock. I had been staring into the darkness for some time.

Lee had worn nothing fake in his life. Were those jeans really fake? Could it be he was telling me the truth? I had been upset in the prison because I thought he was lying to me again. What if he had been telling the truth? I shook my head and whispered in the darkness.

"No, it's not possible. In fact, it's impossible."

Lee had never touched the jeans in the courtroom, they had been nowhere near him and therefore how could he have known they were fake?

Lying bastard. I thought.

I played the court scene over in my mind from

when the court clerk had passed the jeans to the jury. The man from the lab told us he had found not only gunshot residue on the jeans but also Lee's DNA. I could see the barrister's smug grin as he declared the robber's jeans and the jeans recovered from Lee's flat were the same. He was guilty.

I remember the exact moment that I thought that too, the one who loved him with all her heart. He was the father of my son and yet on that day, at that precise moment, I would have said he was guilty. Why did I think that? There was only one answer. It was the jeans.

I knew the police have been planting evidence ever since the days of Robert Peel, but surely not in this case. Why would they? It wasn't as if Lee was some sort of crazed serial killer or a Mafia hitman. He was a petty criminal, a dealer, a bit of a nuisance and a jack the lad, but surely the police wouldn't have wanted him off the streets that badly?

My head was spinning as I walked out of the bedroom at five-fifteen in the morning. I stepped quietly down the stairs and walked into the kitchen. I clicked on the kettle and spooned a heaped teaspoon of Nescafe into a mug. I watched the kettle as it boiled.

It was those bloody jeans. Take those jeans out of the equation and the police and the prosecution had nothing. Lee didn't have an alibi, by his admission he was 'on his own' all day, at home, but there was no ID parade, no fingerprints, nothing, just a tip-off from a snitch and those bloody jeans. They had even searched his house looking for stolen items from the raid, but hadn't found a thing. Lee would be in the clear and if it hadn't been for those jeans, I doubt whether the case would have even come to court.

I turned on my computer. Whilst it booted up, I made another coffee, then typed Google into the search bar. I sat at the computer for three hours.

It was another three days before Lee called. He said he had given me time to cool off and asked if I would visit again.

"I'm sorry," he said. "I promise I won't mention the case again. I'll do my time and I'll be on my best behaviour and I promise I'll be out before you know it."

And he told me about Oscar, how he didn't want him to visit too often, because he didn't want to 'normalise' prison. At last, we were singing from the same hymn sheet.

"I agree," I said. "Birthdays and special occasions."

"Exactly," he sounded relieved. "It will be better for him in the long run. I don't want him to grow up thinking his dad is some sort of hero."

"Don't worry," I replied, "there's no chance of that happening."

Two weeks later, I was back at Long Lartin. I left Oscar at home and drove across the country to the prison. I had put on a classical CD, turned the music down low and spent the three hours thinking. On arrival, they told me that Lee had been on good behaviour and that it would be an open visit in the communal visiting area. After the security formalities, they led me through.

A prison officer pointed to a table. A few minutes later, Lee joined me, beaming like a Cheshire cat. He reached across and placed his hands on top of mine. A warm shiver ran the length of my spine. I didn't pull away. His touch was causing the chemicals in my body to react, and it was not unpleasant.

He spoke first. "I'm sorry."

"For what?" I questioned. "You haven't done anything yet."

He grinned. "For the last time, I just... "

He seemed to hesitate; he didn't want to say anything that might set me off again.

"I'm going to do my time. Only that. I hate it here; believe me, I never want to come back."

He spoke as if he was talking about a couple of weeks. He had been sentenced to fifteen bloody years and even with good behaviour, he'd be banged up for seven or eight.

"Will you wait for me?"

"What?"

"I've heard that you've divorced Pablo."

I nodded. I was a little surprised that he had found out. I felt a sense of shame that I had failed to hold a marriage together for the sake of my sons.

"I'm sorry," he said.

Who was he kidding?

"No, you're not."

"I am, really I am."

I shook my head. "Stop it, you're not. You're over the moon. Be honest with me for once."

He laughed and squeezed my hands. He said nothing, but I knew. We talked about Pablo, about how and where the marriage had gone wrong. He told me that if he had been my husband, he would have worshipped me like a queen, how he would have done everything in his power to make sure our marriage had been the greatest union ever.

"You had your chance to do that," I said.

"We all make mistakes," he replied, "and that was the biggest mistake of my life. I wish I could turn the clock back."

And I believed him. I looked into his eyes and they were almost dreamy, like a teenager in love. And we talked like teenagers in love. I forgot about everything and everyone around me, the criminals and their visitors. He was careful not to mention the robbery and those fake jeans. The robbery... that was another one of his big mistakes.

It was only right that I should bring the subject of the jeans up; I was waiting for the right moment. It came about fifteen minutes before the end of the visit.

"Seven years," he said, "eight at the most and then I'll be out and I'll go straight and get a good job and as soon as I get enough money together I'm down on one knee and I'll be asking you to spend the rest of your life with me."

I raised an eyebrow. "Seven or eight years?" I questioned.

"Yeah."

"That's a long time."

"Not in the grand scheme of things."

"It's still a long bloody time, Lee."

He sank back in his chair and let out a sigh.

"What can I do, Cookie? They ain't gonna let me out any sooner."

"They will if you win an appeal."

"What?" he said.

"An appeal normally takes between eighteen months to two years."

I had floored him. I was quite pleased with myself. He wasn't expecting that at all. He was almost speechless.

"I've been studying the process, and I think you have a case."

"What?"

"Tell me about those jeans," I said. "How did you know they were fake?"

He threw his arms up in the air. "I just did."

"Well, Lee, you are going to have to come up with some better shit than that, because there's no High Court Judge in the land ever going to release you because you say, 'I just did.'"

I edged forward in my seat and lowered my voice. "And more importantly, how do you know that the man in the CCTV footage wasn't wearing fake Stone Island jeans, too?"

He thought for a few seconds. "Because—"

"Yes?"

"Because they looked too good."

I wagged my finger at him. "Again, sir," I mocked, "you'll have to come up with a whole lot better shit than that to convince the judge or even two or three judges that you are innocent and you deserve to walk free. Those CCTV images were poor and you can't prove those jeans were real any more than you can prove the ones in court were counterfeit." I leaned back in my seat. "But if there was a way... "

It was a defining moment, the moment that he finally realised I was taking his claims seriously.

"You believe me?" he said.

I shook my head. "I didn't say that, I said that perhaps you might have a case for an appeal if you can prove those jeans were planted... and that they are fake... and the ones that we saw on the armed robber at the jewellery store were the real deal. Because, from where I am standing, if you can prove that, then the police have an enormous case to answer."

I asked him about the tip-off. Someone had given them Lee's name.

"Why would someone do that?" I waited.

He admitted that he may have handled some of the stolen watches. That was the only thing he could think of. He didn't know who the snitch was. The police hadn't told him.

He had handled the stolen goods from the robbery. Although I knew Lee had been involved in shifting stolen property in the past, it didn't automatically qualify him as an armed robber. There was no proof. They had found nothing in his flat apart from the jeans.

"I think you have a case for an appeal, although you understand I'm not a lawyer yet," I said.

Lee let out a long breath. "Right... right, yes." And then his face fell. "But who will take it on?"

We discussed the practicalities, a solicitor, the costs, possibly even a barrister.

"I can't afford a toilet cleaner, let alone a lawyer," he said. "I've been banged up here for months and not earned a cent."

I couldn't quite grasp that. "You must have some money pushed to one side, Lee."

He nodded. "A few grand here and there, nothing more."

"And your car? What's that worth?"

"Another ten grand perhaps."

A prison officer shouted that visiting was over.

"It's a start," I reasoned. "It's better than nothing; surely a lawyer will look into the case for a decent down payment?"

Within five minutes, I found myself outside the prison gates.

I had more thinking time on the drive back home. I was planning it out in my head. When I arrived in London, I made straight for school... just made it. I picked Oscar up and wondered whether to burden him with where I had been and what we had discussed. I decided not to.

For once, the boys were little angels and were in bed and sleeping before eight o'clock. I poured myself a small glass of wine and settled down at the kitchen table with my notepad and pen.

I made copious notes, compiling all the evidence (or rather the lack of it), the plus points for the police and the prosecution and the plus points for Lee. I kept coming back to the jeans. Could the police really have planted them in the flat? Had they been so bent as to plant some of his DNA onto the denim material, too? I chewed the end of the pen, eased back in my seat and looked up at the ceiling.

It wouldn't be so hard, I thought. *They could have dragged the fake jeans through Lee's bed, they would undoubtedly pick up something.*

I remembered back to the trial. They had matched up pubic hair. Easy. I logged into Google. *Circumstantial Evidence.* I wanted a definition; I was new to this game. A page on Google told me that 'the evidence relies on an inference to connect it to a conclusion of fact.'

They mentioned an example, such as a fingerprint at the scene of a crime. It was becoming clear to me. A fingerprint at the shop, for example, would prove that Lee had been at the shop at some point in time, but not necessarily at the time the crime was committed, because he may have been in that same shop, coincidently, some days or weeks earlier to buy something.

I was getting it now. It said that direct evidence was worth so much more in court because it directly linked the perpetrator to the crime with no additional evidence or inference. A positive ID by one of the staff, for example. It said that circumstantial evidence allows for more than one explanation. Exactly. The jeans found in his flat didn't pin him to the jewellery shop at the time of the raid. Or did they? The gun shot residue. That was fairly conclusive and that worried me.

I took a long sip of wine. The alcohol kicked in immediately and I relaxed. The police had made a huge issue of the Stone Island jeans; about how rare and expensive they were and that just a small percentage of the population wore them. The jeans they had presented to the jury were the exact colour and style as the ones the armed robber had worn. I remember looking at the jury and could almost see the light bulbs going on in their heads as they studied the jeans and the CCTV footage; they looked across at Lee and put two and two together to make five. I read on.

'Different pieces of circumstantial evidence, ie more than one, may be required.'

What? But all they had on Lee were those damned jeans. Take the jeans away and they had nothing. Google search told me that the more pieces of circumstantial evidence would likely strengthen the case against the individual and that 'one piece of circumstantial evidence on its own is not normally enough to convict.'

I read further down the page about reasonable doubt. The article described reasonable doubt, and read, 'there must be clear and convincing evidence of what the person has done and circumstantial evidence alone may not be enough to convict.'

I read the article over again and then clicked on more. They were all saying the same thing: that one piece of circumstantial evidence is not normally enough for a conviction. I tried to put myself in the jury's shoes.

The prosecution had put it plain and simple; they were rare jeans; it would have to be a huge coincidence that he and the robber had worn similar jeans. It was possible, the barrister had said, but how did the defendant explain away the gunshot residue found on those very same jeans found in his flat?

23

CIRCUMSTANTIAL EVIDENCE

By now I was doing the dissertation for my Master's degree, and my days were full. Nevertheless, I went to university the next day to find Law books relating to circumstantial evidence. I also managed to pin one of my lecturers down to a coffee date, where I quizzed him on it.

He told me, "Circumstantial evidence is not always a bad thing but prosecution lawyers and subsequently the jury can sometimes think it's the be-all and end-all of a case. If the prosecution bangs on about it enough, it's almost acceptable to ignore the lack of physical evidence and disregard that fact altogether."

I took him into my confidence and told him about a friend and neighbour of mine who I thought had been hard done by. I mentioned the jeans and the gunshot residue that he had been convicted on. I didn't say that Lee thought the jeans were fake because we couldn't prove that yet. He told me that, on the balance of probability, he wouldn't have thought a jury should have convicted on one piece of circumstantial evidence.

"That's quite rare," he said. "But then again, the gunshot residue is fairly damaging. Unless the defendant could prove he was a member of a gun club or been on a recent shoot in the country, then his lawyer would have been up against it." He laughed. "Is your friend black?"

It was a strange question.

"Yes," I answered. "But what has that got to do with it?"

"Everything," he replied. "A pheasant shoot in the Shires is the preserve of the white upper classes, not the sort of venue you'd find a working-class black man from London."

I could see what he was getting at. "He's banged up for fifteen years," I said.

He shook his head. "Hard luck. And yet the prisons are full of hard-luck stories, innocent people jailed because of one piece of evidence presented cleverly by a well-paid barrister and to be honest with you, the more I think about it, the more I think your friend is going to struggle to prove his innocence."

After our coffee, I was filled with a determination to help Lee and, within a few days, I had convinced

195

myself to at least try it, to see if I could come up with enough material to warrant an appeal to the High Court.

I received a card from Lee a few days later. He expressed his undying love for me and told me everything I wanted to hear. Two nights later, he called me. I told him about my research on circumstantial evidence and the coffee with my lecturer. He listened while I hardly came up for air.

"So, to convict you on just one piece of circumstantial evidence may give you a good reason to appeal."

I heard him take a deep breath. "Those jeans weren't mine, Cookie."

"That doesn't matter, the point is—"

"The point is, you're not listening to me," he interrupted. "Those jeans weren't mine, never had been. They have never covered my arse and if we are going down the route of an appeal, we are going to tell anyone who is listening that those coppers were bent and planted fake evidence."

"But, Lee, circumstantial evidence is—"

"I hear you and you are right; I was unlucky to get banged up on one piece of evidence, but it was fake, babe. They planted those jeans, they weren't mine."

My immediate thought was, why hadn't he mentioned this at his trial? And yet I sensed why. Getting someone in the legal profession to take on an appeal was going to be tough enough, but getting them to take up a case where we were going to accuse the police of deliberately planting fake evidence was a whole different ball game.

I soon got into a routine of visiting Lee every fortnight. We discussed every aspect of the case and agreed that I had to see a barrister, take advice, find out the costs and the exact process. It was important to know whether we had enough reason to be granted an appeal, let alone win it.

I was back on Google that same evening. I typed into the search bar, 'find a London barrister, costs.'

Holy shit! I didn't expect that. I couldn't believe what I was reading.

'Currently our junior BARRISTERS charge between £250-£300 per hour and the most senior members charge up to £600 per hour, depending on the circumstances of the case.' I read on to discover it clearly stated that they would consider only their most senior members for representing a case at the Court of Appeal. £600 an hour!

For fuck's sake.

I reached for my wine glass. It was ridiculous. How could anybody justify that sort of money?

I searched for more firms but the costs were very much of a muchness. Some barristers wanted a ten-hour down payment just to look over the case, with no guarantee that they would take the job on. Six thousand pounds, with the possibility of a 'thanks, but no thanks.'

Lee telephoned that evening. I gave him the bad news.

"Fucking hell, babe, that's crazy."

"It gets worse," I told him. "After ten hours looking over the case, then they charge preparation time and research, and that doesn't include meeting you or even time in court."

I had written some conservative calculations. I estimated taking his case to the Court of Appeal could cost anything up to £50,000 and I quoted a real case cost, where a defendant was reclaiming his costs of £71,000 because he had won.

"And even though he had won his appeal, the judge refused his appeal for costs."

"You have got to be kidding me?"

I wasn't. Every spare hour I could find, I spent researching the appeal process. I read everything I could find relating to court cases dealing with appeals.

As a second-year Law student, I had completed the Criminal Law module; I read we needed a barrister to present the appeal to the judge. That was the key problem because I knew writing an appeal was long and complicated and there was no way Lee or I could afford the sort of money needed.

I had contacts now with the country's top QCs; I had done a mini-pupillage with both respectively (at the Jill Dando trial and the New Cross Fire enquiry) and they liked me. I contacted them for help; this was no time to be shy. I met one, Philip, for coffee, which turned out to be a drink in a wine bar. I came straight to the point and told him about Lee, what my relationship with him was and his claim that he was framed.

Philip loved a rough and tumble with the police but said he wouldn't be able to take it on. However, he was willing to put me in touch with someone who could work pro bono; a Latin phrase that means, *for the public good.* Certain professionals, legal people included, undertake to volunteer their services for those in the community who are unable to afford them. I read that some legal firms even dedicated a special week each year, where their staff are available free. That's all I wanted to hear, and to have that contact.

Philip introduced me to a Junior Counsel, Jeremy Ward-Rice, who wanted to make a name for himself. He was known to work pro bono occasionally, so I reckoned if I sweet-talked him, things might work out. I could only try.

Jeremy was two or three years younger than me, but with an air of confidence. His three-piece suit looked like it had cost more than I could earn in a year. He knew exactly why I was at his chambers. Philip hadn't disguised the fact that I was desperate for him to work pro bono.

He ordered coffee and we exchanged pleasantries. I looked for some common ground, but there was none. I mentioned where I had gone to school and where I had lived, but he had grown up in Epsom, near the racecourse and attended Eton School. As soon as he looked at his watch, I went for the jugular and told him about the jeans and Lee's claim that the police had planted evidence.

He was shaking his head. "Really," he said. "Accusing the police of fitting someone up is a serious accusation."

"I know."

"So you'd better give me something good, otherwise it's a non-starter."

I opened my briefcase and reached for the folder. I slid it across the desk and spoke at the same time. He read and I kept talking. After a minute or two, he held up his hand and I got the message.

He read in silence before saying, "The jeans. What about the jeans? Can you prove that the robber's jeans were genuine and the ones presented to the court were fake?"

I hesitated. "Not yet... but—"

He held up his left hand, returned to the documentation, and read on. After what seemed like a lifetime, he spoke. "Okay, some good news and some bad news." He smiled at me. "Which would you like first?"

"The bad news," I said without hesitation.

He stood up and paced the room. My heart was beating so hard in my chest I was convinced he could hear it.

"Well, you have something," he said, "but not enough to convince me, and certainly not enough to convince a judge that your boyfriend has suffered a miscarriage of justice."

Blunt and to the point. I sighed and sank into the chair.

He continued. "But you might have something that may make a judge sit up and take notice if you do a lot more work on it."

I dared to believe he hadn't refused me. "So the good news is that if I do more work, you will present my case?"

He nodded as he sat down, and I grinned. I returned to earth when I saw his serious expression, an uneasy feeling enveloped my body.

"What?" I asked. "What is it?"

He eased himself further back into his oversized chair. "There's a little more bad news."

I furrowed my brow. "Tell me."

"If you do your homework and I like what I see, then I'll present the case to the judge, but I have to warn you I'll only give you one more chance to get it right, this isn't an open book and I'm a busy man."

"Yes, yes, of course I will."

I was already standing, reaching across the desk to shake his hand; he didn't give me his in return.

"Barristers don't shake each other's hands, it's beneath them."

"Oh yes," I said as I pulled my hand back, remembering that it was still one of the few traditions passed down through the centuries in the profession.

"Thank you so much."

I made my way over towards the door, conscious of his time and a little embarrassed that I hadn't remembered the handshaking code.

As I reached for the door handle, he spoke. "I'll present the case, but you will have to write up the case for appeal."

I turned to face him. "You've got to be kidding me?"

He wasn't. His face never flickered as he chewed on his bottom lip and shook his head from side to side.

"But—"

"I'll present the case pro bono, but don't think for one minute I'm going to work the best part of a week free to write the bloody thing up. That's your job."

I walked towards his desk. "No, no, no. I can't do it. I haven't got the experience."

"Yes, you have, and you can. You're a law student, a bloody good one, because I've just seen what you are capable of. I'll apply for a hearing date straight away, so you'd better get started."

Just as I was about to offer more objections, he looked at his watch again. I got the message, left it at that, and made for the door.

Don't push your luck, I thought; *at least he is going to represent Lee.*

"Oh, one other thing," Jeremy caught me by surprise.

I turned around to see him twiddling a Mont Blanc pen between his fingers. "When you write the appeal, make sure you don't give them everything."

"I, I don't understand."

"Think of it as writing a chapter of a book. You don't want to give the reader too much information, otherwise they will know the entire plot and there'll be no point in turning the next page. Do you understand?"

"Actually, yes... I think I do."

And I did.

"A lot of barristers make the mistake of telling the judges too much, we need to hook and reel them in, tease them, make them curious, only that or we won't be able to land the catch until we get it to court. That's your job when you write the appeal, to cast your line and entice them. My job will be to bring it in once we get there."

"Thanks," I said. "Thank you very much. I won't let you down."

"I know you won't," he replied. "That's why I've agreed to work with you."

24

ALL STATIONS GO ...!

I knew the jeans were the key to the case and, although I sincerely believed Lee in that there were two different pairs of jeans, at this stage we couldn't prove it. I told myself not to worry too much about it, remembering Jeremy's instructions that we shouldn't give too much away in the grounds of appeal. And yet I needed to do something, needed to come up with hard evidence that would set Lee free. How the hell was I going to do that?

A few weeks later, I got a call from Jeremy. We had a hearing date. I couldn't believe it.

The timing was perfect too. After three years of Law School, my Master's Degree and one year on the Bar Course, I was waiting to start my pupillage.

"The hearing will be in the spring," he said. "We

have five months to prepare."

"Excellent."

"Don't let me down."

"I won't."

I couldn't wait to tell Lee. At last, this felt as if it was really happening.

25

A BOLT OUT OF THE BLUE

When I met up with Lee on my weekend visit to Long Lartin, I was excited to tell him about Jeremy, his new barrister, and that he had agreed to work pro bono. I said we had a major problem with the jeans but that Jeremy said we'd be able to get the CCTV footage of the robbery and, if we could get an expert to enhance the footage, we might pull something together. When I told him the barrister had asked me to prepare the grounds of appeal, I puffed out my chest. (I didn't think I needed to mention that I had no choice!)

His reaction wasn't what I expected; he appeared to be on another planet.

And then he came out with it. "I think we should get married."

"What?"

"I can't wait; I want to marry you as soon as possible."

At first, I thought he was joking. I hadn't mentioned marriage since he turned me down that leap year almost twelve years ago, the same year Oscar was born, with the lame excuse of being too young and – although I imagined we would be married one day when he got out – that wasn't what he was proposing at that moment.

"I've made enquiries and it can be done."

"What?" I said.

"Get married in prison," he said.

Closing my eyes to reel me back in from thoughts of barristers, evidence and appeals to what Lee was suggesting, I almost fell off my seat.

"Here in prison!" I exclaimed. "You have got to be kidding!"

That horrified me; it was the worst place in the world to get married.

"Yes, calm down. I have spoken to the vicar. He's a delightful man and they've got a chapel and everything. There would be no mention of the prison on the marriage certificate, if that's what you're thinking."

It wasn't what I was thinking at all. I just couldn't imagine a wedding in this place, with everyone looking on; the prison guards with all those doors, locks, and keys. My mind did a full circle and came back to the appeal; didn't he know it was the most important thing in his life at the moment? This wedding would not happen.

"You're mad, Lee. What about witnesses? Were you thinking of a couple of your favourite screws? It's not my idea of happily ever after, a prison full of murderers and rapists."

"Just think about it," he said. "I want to marry you and I can't wait any longer."

I looked into his eyes. They were moist and sad looking. He had meant every word and, although he tried to make it sound romantic, all I could think of was the venue and how vulnerable I would feel surrounded by screws and criminals! How would that bode for a long-term relationship?

He told me it would be okay, that he had talked with the prison chaplain and that we could have up to seven visitors as long as the prison was given the names a month beforehand.

The more he talked, the more I didn't want to listen.

Is this man for real? I asked myself.

Lee carried on, oblivious to my disbelief. He couldn't wait. He didn't want to risk losing me again. All I had ever wanted to hear was those words, 'Will you marry me?' but not in here, not in this criminal-infested shithole, for fuck's sake; terrorists and paedophiles were walking around. What was he thinking of? He talked about nothing else for the hour. I tried to bring up details I needed for the grounds of appeal, but he was obsessed with marrying me. He tried to counter all my objections and, if I'm honest, he sounded almost convincing. Almost.

But I was having none of it and towards the end of the visit, I could feel myself losing my temper. I thought about the countless hours I had put into the grounds of appeal, nights when I'd fallen asleep at the computer and here he was, not listening to a word I had to say.

The guard shouted that visiting was over.

He reached for my hand. "At least think about it, Cookie."

I got to my feet. "I *have* thought about it."

"You have?"

"Yes, and if you think I'm ever going to get married in a prison then you have another think coming."

He looked stunned. "Please, Cookie, I want to marry you."

"Over my dead body!"

I'd driven about fifty miles after I left before my anger subsided. Ever since I had met the man, I wanted to marry him. I pulled the car over into a service station to calm down as tears welled up in my eyes as the remorse and guilt kicked in.

How could I have been so selfish and what must it be like for him, in there, 24 hours a day? I went over the questions in my head.

Here I was, worried about wearing a nice dress in the shadow of prison bars with a few prison guards looking on.

Of course I wanted to get married, but not here, not like that. When I allowed my imagination to get the better of me, I envisaged a wedding in the Caribbean on a white sandy beach with the warm clear blue waters lapping the shore. If that couldn't happen, then at the very least, a wedding in my own church just a few miles down the road with our family and friends in attendance. But, I pulled back from my dreams with the reality of the present. After all, it was Lee I would marry, not the prison guards, and I was firmly fixed on the fact that he was an innocent man. I was sure it must be hell for him in there, knowing they had fitted him up. He must have summoned up all his courage to even mention it and I'd thrown it all back in his face.

Before I got out of the car, I cleaned my face as best I could and trudged into the huge cafeteria area. With a strong coffee in front of me, I located the prison number on my mobile and pressed call. I had to talk to him. I lied through my teeth, told them it was a matter of life and death and that I had to speak to Lee; I even broke down and cried, which gave my request more authenticity. Lee was asked to call me back. After fifteen minutes, my phone rang.

"Hi, babe, what is it? They told me you sounded distressed. What's wrong?"

"Yes."

"Yes what? I asked if you were okay."

"Yes," I repeated.

"Cookie, please, you're talking in riddles, I—"

"Yes, I'll marry you."

There was silence.

"Did you hear me?

"I did, of course I did. You'll marry me in prison?"

"Yes, yes, yes, so you'd better plan it before I change my mind."

26

'MY VERY BEAUTIFUL WIFE'

On the next visit, there were fleeting references to Lee's appeal. We talked of very little else except the wedding. Would they search me? Could I wear a wedding dress? In the recesses of my mind, I remembered Lee had said we would be allowed seven guests. Who would we ask to be witnesses? Where would we hold the ceremony? Would there be photos and some sort of reception afterwards? I certainly didn't want photos of us posing next to a prison officer or with Lee in handcuffs.

The visit flew by and still I had more questions than answers. It was frustrating because I had so much to do relating to the appeal.

Apparently, the prison had hosted weddings before. It was almost normal and it would be okay,

Lee had said, but I didn't want my big wedding day tainted by the 'environment'.

Lee gave me the contact details to liaise with the prison chaplain, who would deal with the preparations.

Yes, we could take photos, the chaplain told me; yes, we could have seven attendees and he reminded me to give him a list of guests a month beforehand. No, we couldn't have a reception in the prison and, being an armed robber; they wouldn't let Lee out to a wedding lunch at a hotel! But we could have our own choice of music playing as I entered the chapel.

We set a date, and the preparations began.

I didn't want to wear white; I had already had a white wedding, so that didn't seem right, but I wanted it to be special. After all, I was marrying the love of my life in prison and I would do my best to make it feel like a fairy-tale for us both. The more I thought about what we were doing, the more I thought a girl couldn't show any more commitment to her man than marrying him in *the nick!*

I had two favourite artists, Mariah Carey and Luther Van Dross. Luther's songs had been our songs in the early days and, while Lee was inside, Mariah Carey kept us going.

I knew the exact song I wanted; every time I thought of it, tears welled up in my eyes. It was perfect.

The night before we left for my big day, I went to see my dad. I couldn't put it off any longer. I knew what he would say and didn't want any negativity surrounding the event. It was out of respect for him I went to see him at all. I told him I was getting married, but I wasn't looking for his approval. He didn't look up from the table where his glass of whisky sat.

"Thank you for letting me know," he said flatly.

I waited.

He had told me years before that Lee would never change when he'd said, 'You can't make a silk purse out of a pig's ear.' My father liked to talk in riddles. I was his daughter and by now he knew arguing or trying to tell me the error of my ways would only make things worse. He looked resigned. I knew exactly what he was thinking, that his daughter would learn the hard way. He knew all about Lee's criminal past, what had landed him in jail, and that I was helping him appeal his conviction. He didn't approve of any of it. When he sent my brother and I to boarding school all those years ago, I am sure, like most parents who make that sort of sacrifice for their children, he did so, hoping we would have better opportunities than he did. For a father, a daughter is special, one to cherish and protect and what a father dreams and prays for is that his beloved baby girl will choose a life partner who will be their soul mate, one who will provide for them and protect them.

My father had arrived in England on Friday, 22 June 1956 in the Windrush. He arrived on MV Colomie from Trinidad to Le Havre and disembarked at Plymouth, travelling by train to Paddington Station. Initially, like most people from the Caribbean, he lived in South London but later moved to the leafy Surrey suburbs, where he met my mum. Sometimes in life, if you want to change your trajectory, you need to change your environment and with it your perspective. I am sure even in his worst nightmares, he never believed his only daughter would marry a criminal.

I could tell he was devastated by my announcement because he never said another word. When he turned to the whisky bottle and poured himself another generous measure, I knew it was time to leave.

My mother was to fly in from Scandinavia and give me away. She was not at my first wedding so it was only right that I should invite her to my second, even if it was inside a prison! My parents had not spoken to or seen each other since she left when I was five years old and my father had done his best to raise me and my brother. I hadn't seen or heard from my mother either but, as an adult, I had made an effort to rekindle our relationship. It was never going to be a normal mother/daughter bond. But, I looked forward to including her in my wedding celebrations.

It surprised but delighted me that Lee's family agreed to come to the ceremony. This was the only time they visited the prison. It made Lee's day.

I had booked a hotel for the wedding party and we arrived the evening before the big event. I'd had my hair done and slept without moving so that not a strand would be out of place. I woke up early on my wedding day. I hummed to myself and closed my eyes as the warm water from the shower relaxed me.

My soon-to-be sister-in-law did my makeup before I slipped into my dress. It was pure silk; everything was silk, even the veil which I had made myself. My dress was gold interlaced with a turquoise green thread, cleverly mixed twill that glimmered when I moved. My sons were suited and booted in stunning suits with contrasting waistcoats, everyone looked beautiful.

The priest had a tape of the song for my entrance and I had two platinum rings with diamonds for both of us. It was perfect and as real as it could be. I had waited nearly twelve years for this moment and it was going to be everything I had dreamed it would be, and it was.

I blocked out the opening and closing of gates as if they weren't there. As I waited to make an entrance into the chapel, Mariah's clear, angelic voice rose above the beating of my heart. It was really happening. I was really here and I was about to be married. The song 'My All' could have been written for us. I waited for the introduction and the first verse to finish, then I made my entrance, I felt goose bumps as Mariah sang, *I'd give my all for your love tonight* – the words, which I could have written myself, made the hairs on my arms stand up on end.

Here I was, a forty-year-old woman, with tears

welling up in my eyes as the chaplain took us through the marriage ceremony. I meant every word I said, and Lee knew it. He looked so handsome, so vulnerable, but so happy and secure.

I had booked a table at a pleasant hotel restaurant in the village, where we went for a meal to celebrate. Our families were there so, even though the groom was missing, it was as if he was there too. I knew the deal, and I had accepted it. We were now husband and wife.

A few days later, our wedding photos were developed – not a prison bar in sight. They were truly beautiful; it had been a wonderful day. Even better, there was a letter in the post. It was from Lee.

My very beautiful wife,

When I awake tomorrow, it will be roughly 36 hours before I see you again and I am filled with complete and utterly magical sense of love and joyous anticipation. I want to try and convey to you how I feel towards you since we were married. I feel so enormously privileged, quite unnaturally blessed with good luck and God's blessing in a pure and untouched way. I find my present emotional and physical state of being somewhat alien, confusing and yet devastatingly clear and comforting. With my hand on my heart and swearing to the absolute truth in the face of God, I can make this statement that whether Mariah Carey, Beyonce Knowles, in fact any women that I have ever seen or know of, if they came to me with all their riches, fame and beauty, it could not even begin to compete with the monumentally phenomenal [SIC] physical and emotional "lust" that I "yearn" for you. Your beauty as far as I am concerned placed every other women [SIC] in such a saddening, inadequate, unfortunate position! You have a presence that I can only define as "regal", you are extremely intelligent and as much as you have an above average physical strength, your mental and spiritual strength puts you in a category of fairy-tales and legends!! You have such an enormously kind and precious heart, with the will power and stubbornness of a male! Your hair has the curls, waves, comfort and softness of clouds on a summer's day. Your eyes are clear, honest, truthful, with a hypnotic quality that can have you floating in a state of complete perfection. As for your lips!! You have the most beautifully erotic mouth, with perfect teeth and those full and helplessly alluring lips that seem to be continuously screaming to be kissed. Your neck and shoulders prove that what the Greeks were forever trying to attain with their sculptures and pieces of art, in fact is not a thing of fantasy, is actually a reality, confirmed by you in the flesh! You have the legs and body of a goddess, every part of you is perfection from the erotic flow of your breasts, to your full hips and absolutely perfect arse. Legs that go on forever with flawless lines and perfect proportions.

You are a goddess my darling and you are also my

wife, what more could any man want or ask for. You inspire me in a way too numerous to mention. I am so in love with you Caroline and so proud of you. I have absolutely no doubts about our future, I am totally confident in our ability and loving devotion to each other for our marriage to be fulfilling, exciting and utterly worth the wait.

I love you
Your Husband, Lee

27

GROUNDS OF APPEAL

After the excitement of the wedding, I had less than a month to prepare the details of the grounds of appeal and meet up with Jeremy to take him through everything I'd uncovered. My small house was awash with paperwork, research material and of course literally dozens of study books on Law. Just to make matters even more complicated, I was in the final stages of my studies.

Each stage of becoming a lawyer, Law, Bar and Pupillage was challenging from the start. Every level was more difficult than the previous one. Just when you thought you had given your all to pass the first stage, the next stage was even more challenging.

Along with the others at Bar school, I was being taught how to be a lawyer by lawyers. We were filmed, did role-plays and were taken through the actual Law books that practising lawyers use every day of their lives.

One of our lecturers had written the *Advocates Guide on the Magistrates' Court*. He invited us to come to court with him one morning to see how it was done. We couldn't have been more excited.

At Bar school, I was shown what to wear from top to toe and how to wear my hair. I had to wear a black suit every day, even when just training. No make-up was allowed, no nail varnish, no fancy hairstyles. My hair was pulled back; I was told that it wasn't a fashion show. They were assessing us for our capacity to perform under pressure, for our powers of persuasion, elocution and delivery as well as our cross-examination skills.

We were critiqued at every level. But a pass would never be enough for me. I was a mature student, I had kids, I was competing against younger 'baby barristers.' I would need at the very least to attain the high level Very Competent.

Staying late was normal, and I had to get used to it, along with dinners! I had to join an Inn – there are only four – Lincoln's Inn, Inner Temple, Middle Temple or Gray's Inn. Each one had their own area; beautifully manicured gardens, their own library, church, dining hall, bar and members' rooms. These were exclusive clubs for barristers only. The Inns had been around before the days of King Richard the Lion Heart. Not even solicitors were allowed in our Inns. I

221

joined Lincoln's Inn. The site dated back to 1228 by a Royal Charter of Henry III. The original document is still in the Inn's possession. This charter recorded the gift of the site of the future Inn to Ralph Neville, Bishop of Chichester. I chose this Inn because it reminded me of boarding school; a large, impressive building, of historic importance in equally impressive gardens.

I felt at home here but yet on Call Day, I felt as if I didn't belong. The journey getting to the moment to be 'called to the Bar' had been a dizzy mix of hard work and even harder application to work, of sacrifice and many rejections. But I had no choice. It was a life on the dole or this – RSI is forever – there is no respite. Nothing was going to stop me from succeeding and, despite there being many obstacles to get to this point, I wasn't giving up. My father and brother attended. We were the first to arrive. My dad had just bought a brand new Mercedes and he parked it outside the Great Hall. There were only two parking spaces and we had one. It was a proud moment for all of us. That moment was captured for posterity and the photo still hangs on my office wall.

I was determined to qualify as a criminal barrister and had been accepted at 8 King's Bench Walk, the chambers of Lord Gifford QC, a prominent Human Rights chamber. It was going to be tough but it was surreal too because I could actually picture myself standing in a court, long flowing robes and wig, presenting cases to High Court Judges. I carried that vision with me wherever I went. There wasn't a day that went by where I didn't take a moment out, close my eyes and dare to dream that I could do it.

I stopped watching television, going out, socialising. Everything stopped for me. I had to. I was married, but still very much a single parent with my husband banged up inside. But I wasn't complaining. I knew what I had let myself in for. It was all about focus, hard work, and discipline.

I got up at five every morning and went to bed well after midnight. I taught my body to adapt, told myself that four hours' sleep was more than enough. At weekends, when the boys weren't at school, I allowed myself a lie-in. I slept until six. My books went everywhere with me. After-school activities and sports days, I was still there with the boys, but I wasn't one of the mothers who mingled. The mum's coffee group was well attended, but I wasn't one of the members. I was always in a corner with my head in a book or typing up a page of the grounds of appeal on my laptop.

As a member of one of the four Inn's, I had full access to the library and computers which gave me up-to-date information on all cases. The library was to become my second home and I'd beg babysitting favours from my family and friends. I would look for cases heard in the House of Lords and, if I couldn't find similar facts to the case I was looking for, then I would go for Court of Appeal cases.

There were almost a dozen reference books on how to prepare cases for appeal with working examples. I found a book on Drafting, the 15th edition Oxford University Press compiled by senior barristers and lecturers from The City Law School. I thumbed through the contents page and looked down the list at *Criminal Grounds for Appeal,* because that's exactly what I wanted to know about. I read voraciously and was pleasantly surprised that once I had read a few paragraphs, a chapter, or sometimes the entire book, it sank in.

I read, *'A clear understanding of the procedure of the Court of Appeal Criminal Division is vital to a proper preparation of a grounds of appeal* (mental note to self – visit the Court of Appeal and listen to a hearing.) I attended the M25 Appeal. Both Courtney Griffiths QC and Michael Mansfield QC were representing the appellants. Their poise and delivery flowed; it was pure poetry to hear them deliver point after point on why the M25 convictions were unsafe. When I left the Royal Courts of Justice, I was on cloud nine. That was how to do it, I thought. One day I would be just like them.

It continued, *Archbold's Criminal Pleading and Practice, paragraph 7. 163.*

It gave me the full guidelines. And to be honest, it wasn't difficult, it was black and white, it all made perfect sense and I devoured the knowledge.

It talked about the timetable, then the really juicy bit: Grounds of Appeal.

There is now a requirement for the grounds of appeal to set out the relevant facts and nature of the proceedings concisely in one all-encompassing document.

The Criminal Procedure Rules, r.68.3(r)(b) requires that a notice of appeal must identify each ground of appeal, concisely outlining each argument in support. The submission of the grounds enables the single judge of the Criminal Division, who will first consider whether leave to appeal should be granted, to see the factual and legal basis of the appeal.

The grounds of appeal should therefore be written in such a way as to gain these advantages. Grounds that are adverse to the defendant's appeal should never be submitted with the notice of the grounds of appeal. In other words, only positive grounds of appeal should be submitted.

Following the amendment of the Criminal Appeal Act 1968 by the Criminal Appeal Act 1995, there is only one ground of appeal against conviction, namely that the conviction is unsafe. The act read as follows:-

1. Subject to the provisions of this Act, the Court of Appeal –

(a) shall allow an appeal against conviction if they think that the conviction is unsafe; and

(b) shall dismiss such an appeal in any other case.

Examples that might be relied upon included – Fresh evidence that has come to light.

The Grounds of Appeal must be carefully drafted and properly particularised (ie properly arguable).

They should set out succinctly, but clearly, the criticism that is being raised. In relation to each ground, counsel should explain fully why it amounts to a ground of appeal.

My mind went back to my mini-pupillage at the Jill Dando trial. It happen to be during the week of the forensic evidence, the great QC had disseminated the prosecution's forensic evidence due to lack of continuity, casting doubt in the jury's mind of how the *speck* of gunpowder was on the overcoat worn by the defendant. He had scientific evidence that it could have come from the atmosphere or from several other unrelated sources, but the real issue was the evidential room in the police station where all the evidence was kept together: guns, knives, drugs and clothing and the very real possibility of cross-contamination.

I wondered where exactly the gunshot residue on Lee's jeans had come from. Cross-contamination was a genuine possibility and cases were being won on that issue. All I needed was doubt. And yet, I was leaning more towards the fact that the police had planted the evidence.

But I was hanging onto that magical word – doubt. My grounds for appeal had to sow the seeds of doubt into whoever read it. That was my job. It was as simple as that. The more books and articles that referred to grounds of appeal, the more they seemed to shout out that word. Lee had been convicted by a majority jury. Two members were unsure. My grounds were calling every single member of that jury out. It was saying you were wrong, and this is why.

It went on – *list the grounds numbering them consecutively – then deal with each ground in a logical order – either with the stronger ground first or in chronological order.*

I smiled. '*The stronger one first,*' it said. It made sense. A judge had a duty to read the grounds of appeal, but like a good book, it had to grip him or her straight away.

On each ground of appeal, there must be a clear explanation of what the ground is together with the relevant argument. The ground needs to be explained, reasoned and argued with the facts, the evidence and the law. This is not just to show what is wrong but why it is wrong and what 'prejudice' has been caused as a result.

Then the book showed a perfect example of how a ground of appeal is set out on paper with numbered paragraphs and headings; I asked permission from the head librarian and she allowed me to make photocopies of the most important pages.

Introduction – summary of facts;

The nature of the prosecution case;

The defence case – what the defence was;

The evidence against the defendant – how in broad terms the prosecution sought to establish its case; and

Any significant evidence produced to convict the defendant.

Grounds

Conviction

Sentence

'*Always good to say something about this,*' the book read, '*manifestly excessive and therefore wrong in principle.*'

I made a note in my notebook.

The only evidence linking Lee to the robbery was a pair of jeans, which the prosecution said were rare. We don't doubt that; we don't doubt that the robber pictured in the CCTV footage appeared to be wearing Stone Island jeans. I gulped, took a drink from my plastic water bottle, the type of jeans Lee adores. *A coincidence,* I reassured myself. *Nothing more.*

> *1.   Ground of Appeal against Sentence*

I made another note.

> *In passing sentence of 15 years, the learned judge stated that the length of sentence was largely based on Lee Corey's previous convictions rather than the present offence and accordingly the judge's approach was wrong in law. A sentence of 15 years' imprisonment for a single offence of robbery is manifestly excessive and therefore wrong in principle.*

As I read about the appeal of sentence and the note I had made, I was torn. I wondered whether I should be even mention how excessive the sentence was. This was almost a cop-out because I wanted Lee freed. I wrote it all out and promised myself I would make a quick phone call to Jeremy as soon as I left

228

the library. I had convinced myself that my grounds of appeal would concentrate on the lack of evidence and that by mentioning the severity of the sentence; it was as if we were admitting his guilt.

I had my first argument with Jeremy.

"It needs to go in the Grounds of Appeal," he instructed.

I was walking along the street, just outside the library. "But we might as well admit he did it in the first place if we complain about the sentence. In my mind, we are telling the judge he is guilty."

"It's a plan B, Cookie. We have to face facts that no matter how good your application is, the judge might not be swayed to take it to appeal. Don't forget, you are almost accusing the police of planting false evidence."

"I know, but—"

"But nothing. If you could get six or seven years taken off your husband's sentence right now, would you take it?"

"No, I wouldn't. I want him free. He didn't do it."

"You're kidding yourself, Cookie, you're lying to me. It's a plan B and it needs to go in there."

It didn't sit comfortably with me at all, and yet he was the seasoned barrister and I was the pupil. He would present the appeal to a judge and I reminded myself that I was working for him. He had experience and I had to do exactly as he said.

"How long is the appeal now?"

His words interrupted my thoughts.

"My first draft is forty-nine pages, and that's without the excessive sentencing insert."

"Too fucking long, Cookie."

My God, it was the first time I had heard my handsome, public school-educated barrister swear.

"Twenty-five pages max, and that's it. We need to spike the judge's interest, not bore him to death. It's just one judge from the Criminal Division and we had both better hope he is having a good day and is up for a read. If you hit him with fifty or sixty pages and he's got up on the wrong side of bed, then it's dead in the ditch and you'll have wasted your time."

"I agree," I chipped in. "So why push more pages in relating to the excessive sentence?"

Before I could offer any argument, Jeremy cut me short. He said it wasn't up for discussion and reminded me he was working pro bono. "You'll work on my terms or find yourself another barrister."

"Yes, Jeremy." *Three fucking bags full, Jeremy.*

I'd got the boys to bed early, by seven-thirty, and I'd worked well, condensing the entire document, including the two-page excessive sentencing referral, down to thirty pages of A4. It was still like a fucking dissertation! It was now approaching midnight.

I printed it out and read it through again... paragraph by paragraph, line for line, word for word, more than aware it was this document versus one judge. And yet, when I read it through completely just after one thirty in the morning, I was pleased with it.

It read well. There was only one problem, however. The jeans.

I still couldn't prove that the jeans the police had claimed they found in Lee's flat didn't belong to him. I couldn't prove they were fake and nor could I prove that the jeans in the CCTV footage differed from the ones the police had provided.

That was the sticking point. I remember Jeremy had told me not to worry about it and concentrate on the grounds of appeal. If I really believed Lee, and it was the truth, then we would find a way.

I read it over again. Opening paragraph.

We intend to prove that the jeans found in the Appellant's flat were not the same jeans pictured in the CCTV footage from the robbery.

Wow! What a statement. That was a hook alright. What judge wouldn't sit up and take notice of that and grant the right to appeal? And I believed Lee. I believed him so much but, just like the police gathering the evidence to put a criminal away, there was a problem; proving it. I could believe Lee with all my heart, be 100% convinced, but if I couldn't come up with anything to back up what I was saying then the appeal paper wasn't worth Jack Shit, even though it was worded brilliantly well, (and it was,) I needed to back it up with hard evidence which our barrister could present to the court.

28

NO PRESSURE

I went to bed just after two in the morning; my alarm went off at five. I snoozed twice and was sitting at my computer just after six with my second coffee of the morning, after reading the appeal through again. I made a few amendments and sent it to Jeremy just before seven.

By nine-fifteen, he was on the phone. "It's brilliant."

"What?"

"It's everything I asked of you."

"What?"

"You'll make a great barrister one day."

That was the good news and then he asked, "Of course you can back that up, can't you?"

"Yes," I said without hesitation. "Of course I can."

"You are sure?"

"Yes. You told me you could request a DVD of the CCTV footage from the robbery."

"We're already on it; it should be with you by the end of the week," Jeremy confirmed.

"Great, and I'll need the jeans."

"Sorry."

"The jeans," I repeated. "The pair they presented to the jury, the fake ones. I'll need them."

The silence at the other end of the line turned my blood to ice.

It seemed like an age before he spoke. "You have to be kidding me."

"No, I need to prove that those jeans are fake."

"And you think the police are going to hand over the only piece of evidence they have?"

"Well, why not?" I protested.

"You are not serious, Cookie. Think about it; think about what you could do to those jeans."

"... you mean... " The penny dropped.

"Yes, you could tamper with the evidence, find new DNA, you could do anything to them and that's why the next time you see them will be at the Court of Appeal."

His words had struck me dumb.

"This is what the appeal hinges on," he said. "Tell me you can prove those jeans were fake without examining them in person?"

My world caved in. How had I been so stupid and naturally assumed they would allow me to have possession of the jeans?

I backtracked and lied. "Yes, of course I can. It just would have been easier to prepare the case if I could have seen the jeans."

We exchanged a few pleasantries, and I pressed end call.

Fuck, fuck, fuck, I thought. *Double fuck and shit. How on earth am I going to do that?*

The very next day, I got a letter from Jeremy. He said my Grounds of Appeal would be forwarded to the single judge of the Criminal Division. Jeremy had made a few amendments to the appeal, but nothing too dramatic. No pressure then.

29

MANAGING EXPECTATIONS

At the next visit, I talked the matter of the jeans through with Lee.

"So, I'm sorry, but we can't get a hold of the jeans. They won't allow it. It's against their procedures."

"No?"

He looked a little despondent, but we were still in that honeymoon period and so I tried to remain positive. I explained it was all about the appeal and it was no use worrying about it until the judge had granted leave to appeal anyway. I'd done my best. I repeated to Lee the very word that Jeremy had used: *brilliant.* He reached across the table and stroked my hand.

"I'm so proud of you," he said. "Whatever happens, you'll be the best barrister in the country one day."

I laughed. "Just the petty matter of completing pupillage, Lee, don't get too carried away."

And yet failure wasn't an option; it was about application and hard work. By now I had started pupillage and was shadowing my pupil master, a senior and seasoned barrister who teaches you the ropes. It was all about watching and learning. And I couldn't get enough. I absorbed the camaraderie, the nod and the wink from others in the profession, the air of respect, people knowing your value instead of seeing you simply as a 'mum'. And I enjoyed every minute; in the court room, in the cells taking instructions, the legal research, finding that 'one' legal authority that supported your argument to win your case; discussing the cases with other barristers to gain a different perspective to test your line of thinking or being asked for my opinion from my pupil master so he could assess my progress. I couldn't wait to be allowed to conduct cases myself, under the pupil master's supervision, of course. I recalled the discussions with my fellow pupil barristers; they complained about how tough it was and how long it took to understand unfamiliar concepts. They were much younger than me, their brains were not so full of data and, according to the doctors and scientists, it was far easier for them to absorb and retain information. What was wrong with them? Try being a single working mother with a husband in jail, then come and complain to me.

We drifted off the subject of the jeans for a while and talked about our wedding. Lee asked me about the reception in the hotel and I played it down a little.

"It wasn't quite the same without the groom," I said.

He told me he'd make it up to me once he was out. "After the appeal," he said.

More pressure.

It was time to manage his expectations.

"Lee, you realise that the granting of an appeal depends on just one Criminal Division Judge?"

"Yeah, babe."

"And we hope that not only has he had a great day when he reads it, but that he is also in the mood for a good read."

Lee raised an eyebrow. "Is it long?"

"Six thousand words."

"That's long."

"Thirty pages of A4. As I've said, we have to hope the judge is having a good day, otherwise he'll skip through it, miss the point of it all, and chuck it in the bin."

"But it's good, yeah? The barrister said it was brilliant?"

I nodded. "It can be the best appeal application in the world, but it still depends on one judge."

I played it all down and fleetingly wondered why. But I knew why. It was the jeans, the jeans we wouldn't see until we were standing in front of an appeal judge. It seemed unfair. This was the key to the case, the reason they sent Lee down, and it was a one-sided playing field. There was no doubt about it. And then the worst thought in the world. What if my husband was wrong about the jeans or, worse... lying to me? How could I think such a thing?

He reached for my hand again. "What is it, babe? You're not yourself today."

I did the only thing I could think to do. I burst into tears. A prison guard brought me a box of tissues and I apologised. He looked at Lee with suspicion and I assured him it was nothing he'd said. The pressure cooker had finally blown its top. I was in my 'first six' of pupillage and was attending court daily with my pupil master. It was all too much for me, the work, the reading, that thirty-page appeal and the countless hours of research, shopping, housework and the school run, after-school activities and parent's evenings not to mention the jail run too.

And the loneliness. An empty bed, no husband, no intimacy. Nothingness. I cried buckets, told Lee that life was unfair, the courts were unfair and how on earth did I expect to put his barrister in court with nothing more than a suspicion that a certain pair of jeans weren't the pair of jeans that the police had removed from Lee's flat?

Lee told me not to worry. "We'll work it out, babe."

How? I thought.

Visiting drew to a close. I walked through the series of prison gates to the sound of keys jangling and doors closing. A cheerful prison officer was whistling a theme from a TV show I'd heard before but couldn't place.

The tears had dried but the frustration, anxiety and feeling of hopelessness engulfed me. And yet, I still held on to a strange thought. The grounds of appeal. I expected the judge would throw it out, that was for certain. So, I was worrying about nothing. The application would end up in the judge's bin and the pressure would be off. My husband might not be coming home soon and I had accepted that when I married him. I clutched at straws, told myself it was his fault, his stupidity that had put him where he found himself and I would concentrate on finishing my pupillage and becoming a barrister and we would have a great standard of living when he eventually came home.

I took the phone call just outside London. *Jeremy Barrister* appeared on the phone display. I pressed accept call. This was it. The judge had thrown it out.

"How are you Cookie?"

"Fine, just been to see Lee."

"Really?"

"Yes."

"How is he?"

"So, so, it wasn't the best visit I've ever had with him."

239

A slight pause. "I'm sorry to hear that. Is he looking forward to his appeal hearing?"

It took a second or two for his words to sink in. "What did you say?"

"His hearing."

I could almost see the big stupid schoolboy grin on Jeremy's face. "Did you just say—"

"I did. We have a date. You did it, girl. Your application was fantastic, I told you."

I was stunned into shock. "But... but—"

"Three months' time. Don't you be letting me down. Give me something to knock them dead with."

30

CARLOS GARCIA

Something to knock them dead with. That's what I had to come up with. The obvious place to start was the CCTV footage of the robbery. Surprisingly enough, after Jeremy's phone call, it was with me in forty-eight hours, by special courier, no less.

The footage was crap. I couldn't quite believe that the police had built a case on that evidence alone, but they had, and they had convinced a jury. I remembered looking at the footage in court but paid little attention. I had been fixated on what the prosecution barrister was saying; he'd gone on and on about the Stone Island jeans, and that white, belt buckle patch that was exclusive to Stone Island, about how he was in no doubt that the robber was wearing these designer items and how an identical pair had been found in Lee's flat. It was hardly a coincidence, he'd said, and surprise, surprise, even a little gunshot residue and DNA for added convenience.

I watched the tape again and again. Jeez, it was bad. And yet... as I slowed down the footage and froze the frame, it was plain to see the white belt buckle patch of the Stone Island jeans, only I couldn't make out the writing. It may as well have said Mickey Mouse jeans. How had the police convinced a jury on this evidence? I closed down the computer and sat back to think.

I had to believe Lee. If I couldn't present Jeremy with the evidence that the jeans in the CCTV footage were genuine and the ones the cops had presented, (allegedly recovered from Lee's flat) were fake, then I might as well call it a day and tell my husband to enjoy the next seven or eight years at Her Majesty's pleasure. Because, to be frank, there was nothing else to go on.

I looked at my watch. It had just turned midnight. Too early to head off to bed. I booted the computer up again. The DVD kicked in automatically at the place I had been reviewing. I studied the walk of the robber repeatedly. His gait was like Lee's walk, but there was something that didn't sit right with me. This wasn't Lee. He looked clumsy. Shit, he looked too bloody tall as well. And then I had an idea.

I had read in some crime thriller where the defence had called on a company who specialised in analysing and improving CCTV recordings. I wondered. Was this just a figment of the author's imagination or were there companies out there who specialised in this sort of thing? There must be!

Google brought me thousands of results. I narrowed it down to the English-based companies within a hundred miles of my location and read through the results. I settled on a company from Milton Keynes. Their reviews were excellent, and I liked what they had to say, especially about their experience in court. This was real, this was not crime fiction.

As video forensic experts, we enhance CCTV footage on video recordings from both digital and analogue surveillance systems. Often times, the courts we testify in want to know how to enhance security camera videos. We use non-destructive techniques to preserve the video evidence integrity and pixel quality.

That's exactly what I needed, improved pixel quality, something to show that the jeans in that footage differed from the ones the police had presented in court. I needed to sew doubt in the judge's mind. That magic word. If the judge was in any doubt that the police evidence was flawed, then Lee would walk free. I read more.

We can re-size or scale an image or video to a larger resolution to further identify suspects and can enhance the edge contrast of an image or video.

We use state of the art, software programs and CCTV enhancement tools to help us enhance or clarify the footage; we work with tapes, DVDs or mobile phone footage. We create customised filtering to sharpen the video image and remove video noise for identification and enhancement of the images in the CCTV surveillance video.

I called them the following morning and explained the situation. I told a little white lie and said I was a barrister (it was only a matter of time) and it worked because, suddenly, the guy on the other end of the line got serious. He started selling their services to me.

We made an appointment; he said he would get one of his London operatives to attend the meeting at my place of work. I met him in a café near to Lincoln's Inn, a tall, dark guy, who introduced himself as Carlos Garcia, a forensic CCTV operative. He clearly knew his game and was, I guessed, of Spanish origin. He had told me to bring a copy of the original DVD which he inserted into his laptop. He studied the footage for some time, asked me exactly what it was I wanted to see and have enhanced.

I walked him through, frame by frame, from the moment the armed robber walked into the jewellers, fired the shotgun and left. He was in the shop just short of three minutes. Carlos took notes, smiled, grimaced and sometimes cursed under his breath (in Spanish) and asked me yet again what it was I needed to see. I took a deep breath and eventually came clean, after all, he wasn't a cop; he worked for a private firm.

"The jeans," I said. "I need to prove that they are genuine Stone Island jeans."

He shrugged his shoulders. "Why?"

"It's none of your business, I just do. So tell me, can you do it?"

Carlos was convincing; he said they could enhance the video so much that I would see the lettering on the rivets of the jeans in crystal clear quality. The slight problem was that it would cost me six grand.

I nearly fell off my seat.

"What?"

"It's an awful lot of work and the software we use didn't come cheap. Half up front," he said, "the rest on delivery of the enhanced DVD."

Who was I to argue? I had no choice, so I made the first payment there and then. We sealed the deal on a handshake and as I left the coffee shop; I reminded myself that it wasn't such a big deal. Our barrister was working pro bono. Six grand was all we were going to lay out.

Seven days later, I emailed proof of the second payment and a specialist courier delivered the enhanced DVD three hours later. I took out my laptop, booted it up, and inserted the DVD.

This was good, this was very good. It was like looking at a movie on the screen and there were buttons down the side to zoom in, take single frame capture or record in sections and there were 'save as' buttons where I could send my recordings to a folder of my choice. I fast-forwarded the footage to the critical point. I noticed a 'clip frame' button and could cut the entire footage down to the critical three minutes. As I zoomed in on the armed robber and moved the cursor downwards, I moved a little magnifying glass over the white patch on the back of his jeans. I caught my breath. It was crystal clear,

A PRODUCT OF SPORTSWEAR COMPANY

The real McCoy, surely?

And underneath

STONE ISLAND 44 43 46N 11 07 09E

It was as easy as reading from a magazine. It was six grand well spent. I was now more than confident of proving to anyone that would listen that the jeans the armed robber was wearing at the jewellery store were one hundred percent kosher.

But I had my doubts as I lay in bed and thought about what I had been looking at on the DVD earlier in the day. It was a white patch with writing on, nothing more, and the forgers these days were more than capable of copying something as basic as that. I'd seen the copies close up before, at a market in Bermondsey, where they were selling for forty quid. They looked like the genuine article to me, labels and all, but Lee had steered me away from the Asian man who was trying to convince us they were genuine, the result of a robbery on a warehouse up north.

"Fake," Lee had said.

"You sure?"

He nodded. "Otherwise they'd be selling them for a lot more."

The alarm tune woke me up at five after I had tossed and turned all night. I groaned, convinced that I had set it wrong. I hadn't. I lifted my head from the pillow and made my way slowly down the stairs. I clicked on the kettle and made a cup of coffee. I walked over to my computer, still sitting on the kitchen table, booted it up, logged into Google and typed in the search engine *the difference between fake and genuine Stone Island jeans.* To my amazement, the first result that appeared was a YouTube video.

I pressed play.

31

A SPANNER IN THE WORKS

It was something Carlos, the Spanish CCTV man, had said. The words had come to me through the night. *I could see the lettering on the rivets of the jeans in crystal clear quality.* The rivets. Could it be that the smallest item that made up the jeans could be the very thing the forgers skipped on? The lettering on the rivets; of course. Why would they go to all the trouble for that sort of detail? If the pockets were in the right place and the patches were good and the material was the exact colour, of similar quality and the rivets were the right size and colour, then why go to the trouble of engraving each one? It wouldn't make any sense, would it?

The rivets, that was the key. I sat down, clicked on the *'saved DVD'* file, and pressed play.

Two minutes and seventeen seconds in, I froze the frame. A clear view of the armed robber's backside. The patch on the pocket, two distinct rivets. I zoomed in; right in. The rivet was almost the size of the screen and there it was, two words spanning the circumference of the rivet: STONE ISLAND.

If Carlos had been in the kitchen right at that very moment, I swear I would have kissed him full on the lips. I checked every rivet on the CCTV footage, from the patches and the back pockets to the smaller front pockets and even the small knife pocket on the front left-hand side, just below the belt loops. All rivets with STONE ISLAND circular lettering. Bingo! There was no doubt in my mind, there was no way these could be forgeries.

I finished yet another cup of coffee and found myself light-headed. Too much caffeine perhaps, but the fact was I was absolutely buzzing.

Later on, during a break in proceedings with my pupil master, I tried to get hold of Jeremy. He had been in court when I called, but an hour after my initial call, he rang me back.

I talked him through everything. I told him about enhancing the CCTV footage and the lettering on the rivets and how I could now prove that the jeans worn in the robbery were undoubtedly genuine.

He burst my bubble a bit when he spoke, "So if you can prove those jeans the cops have are fake, then we have a cast-iron case."

"Exactly."

"So, how are you going to do that before we get to court? I've already told you they won't release such critical evidence."

He had caught me on the back foot. I presumed we would just turn up and inspect the fake jeans. Bob's your uncle.

"They won't let you anywhere near those jeans, Cookie."

"But that's wrong, that's so wrong, we should be able to have access to them as well."

"Well, we haven't and you surely don't expect me to go into court blind, Cookie?"

"No, but... I... "

"I need to be sure before I get there, good preparation and solid facts, that's how I work. I'll present the appeal but only if you give me something concrete. It's no good saying we think these are real and these are fake. We have to know."

I hesitated for a moment, struggled for something to say.

His last words brought me back to the present. "You haven't thought this through, have you?"

"No."

"You're nearly there, Cookie, just think it out to the end. Put yourself in my shoes. You wouldn't want to go in there with Jack Shit, would you?"

"Of course not."

"Exactly. Now, I have to go. I have a client meeting in twenty minutes."

He ended the call. He was right, of course. It was a logical solution, not one hundred percent fool proof, but it was our only option. It was Lee who came up with it on the very next visit.

"Go to Bermondsey and pick up a pair of fakes."

Simple.

"Compare them. There'll be something different and then when your barrister is in court, he'll know. Take him a pair of real ones and a pair of fakes, and I guarantee you there will be at least two or three things that don't add up."

I cut the visit short. For the first time, I didn't wait until they threw me out. Lee was protesting but he smiled as I stood up and told him I had to get to Bermondsey. The market was open four days a week Tuesdays, Thursday Fridays and Saturdays.

It was Friday. I had a day off as the jury was out in my pupil master's trial. It was impossible for me to get to the market on a Saturday because of after-school sports. If I didn't leave now, it would be five torturous days until I could pick up the jeans and put my mind at rest.

"I'm not going to have this hanging over me all weekend. I need to get this done today. It's as simple as that."

Lee said he understood. He had no choice.

"What time does the market close?" I asked.

"I don't know," he said. "I think it's around six."

I looked at my watch. It was just after two. I would just make it if I got my skates on.

The Sikh market trader wearing an orange turban at Bermondsey market had surely never held a conversation like this one. I spotted a small pile of the jeans I wanted and walked over to his well-kept stall. "I want a pair of those, please."

"Certainly, madam. What size would you like?"

I shrugged my shoulder. "It doesn't matter."

He looked at me with a confused expression. "What do you mean it doesn't matter, madam?"

"Doesn't matter."

He looked at my waist. "Are they for you?"

"No,"

"Your boyfriend then?"

"Errm, not really."

"Husband?"

I shook my head.

"Then who are they for?"

It was a logical question, but there wasn't really a logical answer. "They are for—"

"Yes, madam?"

"Errrm, my barrister friend, we work together."

"Good." The Sikh breathed a sigh of relief. "At last we are getting somewhere. So what size waist is he?"

"I dunno."

The trader held out his arms to the side and frowned. "You don't know his size?"

"No."

"Well, is he about my size? ... slimmer or fatter?"

"Slimmer."

His brow below his turban line furrowed. "Then that's a problem. I'm a thirty-four waist and that's the smallest we have in the adult size. It's been a busy day; we've sold all the thirty-twos."

"That's okay, I'll take a thirty-four then."

"You sure?"

"Yes."

He raked through the pile while my eyes strained to see if I could make out the writing on the rivets. Too far away. He looked through the pile again.

"I'm sorry madam, it seems like all the thirty-fours have been sold today. We only have thirty-sixes and thirty-eights. If you want to come back on Tuesday, I'll have more."

"No worries," I said. "Thirty-sixes, they'll do."

He threw his arms up in the air. "Madam, we have established that your barrister friend is about a thirty-two inch waist. They would hang off him, he'd struggle to keep them up, come back Tuesday; I'll put a pair to one side for you."

"Doesn't matter, give me those. It's not as if he will wear them."

The look on the stall owner's face was priceless, and I couldn't help smiling. He had now almost given up questioning me and reached for a roll of brown paper. "Forty-five pounds, please."

"Smashing." I took out my purse and counted out the money. "Are they fake?"

He grinned. "No, madam, they are one hundred percent genuine Stone Island, came to me via a friend of a friend who is not entirely honest."

What I said next nearly tipped him over the edge. "I want a fake pair."

"Madam?" he questioned. "Now you surely are taking the piss."

"No, no, not at all. I want a fake pair. Genuine jeans are no good; they must be fake."

I think my market trading friend almost lost it as he ranted about how many years he'd worked on Bermondsey market. He said that in all that time nobody had ever asked for a fake anything. He finished by winking at me, told me that of course they were fakes, otherwise how would he be able to sell them for forty-five quid?

The transaction was completed, and he wrapped the jeans. As soon as I got back to the car, I ripped them open to check the rivets. Then I called Jeremy and told him I needed to see him.

32

PLAIN AS DAY

I think even Jeremy was impressed. He smiled and shook his head as I played back the video of the CCTV footage, zooming in on the lettering of each rivet. I even zoomed in on the smaller rivets of the knife pocket, where the wording was as clear as bottled water.

Speaking like an expert, I told him, "This is where the copiers cut the corners. Unless someone is just a few inches away from the rivets of the jeans, there's no way can they read the writing, so why bother?"

I took him through a repeat performance and at one point; he asked if the man in the video resembled my husband. It was a fair question and a critical one too, because he was asking me categorically whether

I believed the armed robber in the footage was my man.

"Forget the jeans for a second," he said. "If we took the jeans out of the equation, could it be him?"

It was a question I'd asked myself again and again, and this was where I held another ace up my sleeve. I'd watched the footage over fifty times and there was something about the way the robber moved that just wasn't Lee. His build was similar, I had to admit it, but I'd never seen Lee walk like that.

I took a deep breath and spoke. "To be honest with you, Jeremy, I've asked myself that question a thousand times. I've told myself to remain impartial, but the fact is I'm madly in love with my husband and part of me is fully aware that I sincerely want to believe anything that tumbles from his mouth."

Jeremy sat twiddling his fancy pen. He had no intention of opening his mouth. He wanted to know what was coming next.

"The Stone Island jeans concerned me because I know just how much he loves those types of jeans and at any one time he's had several pairs on the go. In his mid-twenties, he wore nothing else, and it seemed too much of a coincidence."

"So when the police recovered a pair of those exact jeans from his flat, you put two and two together."

"Exactly, and then, of course, there was the gunshot residue, to me, that was game set and match."

"He was guilty."

"As the day is long."

"So, what changed your mind?"

"I went to see him in prison. It was a standard visit. We mentioned nothing about being innocent or guilty, never mentioned the robbery in the jewellery store, but as I was leaving, he mentioned those jeans. That's when he looked at me, and believe me, Jeremy, there was sincere honesty in his eyes and he told me that the jeans the cops had presented to the court were fake."

"And he didn't wear fakes?"

I shook my head. "No, he couldn't explain why they were fake. He just said he knew, said he had worn Stone Island since he was a teenager and if anybody knew the brand, he did. He said that there were more fake Stone Island jeans flying around London than there were real ones. So if we could prove that the jeans worn by the robber were real and that the ones presented by the police were fake, then he was off the hook. So I investigated, I invested in the CCTV company and studied the improved footage, the footage I've just shown you. There were two parts to the jigsaw puzzle, and I felt that, when I had seen the engravings on the rivets in the footage, I had completed the first part. I just needed to find a pair of fake jeans, which would prove my theory beyond doubt."

I reached into my bag and pulled out the fake jeans. I couldn't help myself; I broke out into a big, beaming smile as I spoke. "I can't even tell you how excited I was when I looked at the fake jeans. The quality was simply amazing. The material felt as good as a proper pair; the pockets, the patches and the stitching; everything was almost perfect. But then I looked closer and there it was, as plain as day."

I pushed the jeans across his desk and he picked them up, reaching for his glasses at the same time.

"The rivets."

I watched as he focussed in... and then he spoke. "Well, fuck me. I don't quite believe it."

I leaned back in my seat. It was a feeling I had experienced in my school years when a teacher had announced I was top of the class or had won a prize at the riding school's end-of-year prize giving. It was pride. I basked in the moment; it was as simple as that. Despite all the obstacles that had been placed in my way, not to mention the fact that we could not get our hands on the exact item of evidence that Lee had been convicted on, I believed I had cracked the prosecution's theory and blown it wide apart.

He looked again, smoothed his forefinger over one rivet. "But you haven't answered my question."

I hadn't, but I hadn't forgotten either. "The answer is yes, Jeremy, yes he resembles Lee, as much as he is a black man, tall and built like a brick shithouse. But something was nagging me, something not quite right about the way he walked in and out of the shop and then there was the height of the robber."

"Too tall?"

"Yes. The robber was definitely on the tall side, so I asked the experts at the CCTV company to do another check. I had read that by analysing nearby objects, measuring the exact height, they could find out the height of other objects and people around them. They went back to the jewellery shop and measured everything. The counters, how high the clock was on the wall and of course, took the height of the staff who were there at the time of the robbery."

"And?"

They claimed that their assessment of the height of the armed robber would be accurate up to a single millimetre.

"And?"

"They worked out that the armed robber is six feet two."

"And Lee is?"

"A millimetre short of six feet."

"What if it was Lee? What if he was wearing heels, like cowboy boots?"

I laughed. "Don't you worry about that. Lee wouldn't be seen dead in a pair of cowboy boots. He hates them. His brother perhaps, but not him."

Jeremy sank back into his seat. He removed his glasses and placed them on the table. He reached over for his desk diary, made a few notes, and then stood. "Well then, we have twenty-one days to prepare for the appeal."

33

THREE PAIRS OF JEANS

As soon as Caroline, aka Cookie, left the room, Jeremy booted up his computer. He knew he couldn't leave anything to chance and typed in the London markets in the near vicinity of where his nephew, Niles, lived. He picked up the phone, keyed in a number. It was answered immediately.

"Hi, Niles, how are you?"

They exchanged a few pleasantries and then he got down to business. He told his nephew that he was putting £150 into his account and that he was buying him three pairs of jeans. Fake jeans, Stone Island to be specific.

Preparation and planning. That was the key to success.

34

OFF THE CASE

Jeremy called a meeting a week after I left his office. I was even more surprised when I walked into the room and spotted three pairs of black jeans on his desk, neatly piled on top of each other. I knew by his expression that he was about to give me some bad news, only I didn't know what a body blow he was about to deliver, how my weeks and months of hard work were about to be cast aside.

He started by telling me he couldn't handle the appeal, he wouldn't be in court, wouldn't be anywhere near it.

I sat in silence as he held up the first pair of jeans and explained.

"I sent my nephew around a few of the markets. In order to walk into an appeal court, we must leave nothing to chance."

"I understand."

"I wanted to be sure that if, as you say, those jeans we will see for the first time in a couple of weeks are fake, your theory about the missing writing on the rivets is one hundred percent sound."

He reached for the first pair of jeans and pushed them across the desk towards me.

"Look at the rivets."

I picked them up and smiled. There was no writing to be seen.

"And these." He handed the next ones over. "They were the same.

I sensed what was coming next.

"And these." He pushed the last pair over.

I reached for them and my heart sank. I shook my head. The Stone Island writing on each rivet was plain to see. "They're fake?" I asked.

"Forty-five quid from Camden Market."

And before I said what I was thinking, that two out of three was worth taking a chance on, he was pitching his closing argument.

"And if what you say is correct, that the police have planted those jeans, have you ever thought about the unthinkable, that they may have taken the trouble and the expense to go for a proper pair of Stone Island jeans? Can you imagine how stupid we will look? Can you imagine the damage it will do to my reputation when our big argument is blown apart?"

"But I... we... "

"You want me to go in there and accuse the police of planting false evidence on nothing more than your husband's hunch that the jeans he saw were—"

"It isn't a hunch; Lee knows his designer clothes."

"He didn't even touch them, Cookie. He was never closer than six yards to those jeans."

And then the doubts crept in. I picked up the last pair of jeans again, stared at them as if the writing on the rivets would miraculously disappear before my eyes.

"It's up to you now," he said, shaking me from my depressing, miserable thoughts. "I can cancel the hearing or you can go in there and take a chance."

"Me!" I exclaimed loudly. "I can't go in there on my own."

"A wise decision. Then let me cancel it."

"No."

Jeremy looked at his watch. He wasn't in the mood for a prolonged argument.

"You have seven days to let me know. Cancelling it any later won't look good. Sleep on it, Cookie, have a real good think about it but remember, your reputation is on the line too."

35

A WING AND A PRAYER

I never slept more than thirty minutes at a time during that night. When my alarm went off at five-thirty, I didn't have the energy or the inclination to get out of bed and lay for another twenty minutes, convincing myself what a terrible world lay on the other side of my front door. I cursed our barrister for his two-part jigsaw puzzle analogy. There were many more parts than two. I agreed that there was a large part lost in the box's corner, but surely it was worth looking for.

I became a coffee zombie for the rest of the morning and the more the caffeine kicked in, the more the doubts filtered in. The police, had they really planted the jeans? And more so, if they had, were they stupid enough to plant a pair of fake ones?

Surely they would have known that an expert could tell the difference? Or had they?

I had spent six thousand pounds on getting the videos enhanced. Had the Met Police forked out that sort of money? No way, not with all the cuts being imposed on police services. They had looked at the grainy CCTV footage on the shop's cameras and couldn't believe their luck when they picked out that white patch. Lee was known as a flashy dresser, find a pair of Stone Island jeans in his flat and it was enough to sow the seeds of conviction in a jury's mind.

And some things bothered me because I knew Lee wore Stone Island jeans and yet the police found only one pair. Why was that? Had he switched his brand now that he was a little older? Evisu or Armani? I'd heard him mention those brands recently. But...

I wracked my brain. Perhaps in our early days, I was more aware of the exact brands he chose; when we socialised together, a Saturday afternoon in the West End, a decent restaurant that same evening, or perhaps a wine bar in Knightsbridge or Kensington. I needed to know.

I caught up with him on the telephone that same evening. I dropped the bombshell about the barrister not taking on the appeal. Lee cursed and swore when I told him it was all about those jeans.

"The thing is, Lee, it's not over."

"How come?"

"Well, I can't present the appeal until I've finished pupillage, and that's another few months away. We'll have to request another date."

Silence at the other end of the line.

I continued. "But like the barrister said, we can't go in on a wing and a prayer."

"I understand."

"I need you to put a percentage figure on how sure you are about those jeans being fake."

"A hundred percent," he fired back rapidly.

"Get fucking realistic Lee," I said. "You didn't even touch them. In fact, you didn't get within a yard of them. They were in a transparent bag most of the time. For fuck's sake, don't give me that because it's ridiculous."

I'd caught him by surprise. I heard him hesitating before he eventually answered.

"You're right, I'm sorry."

"So think again. From a distance, when you were looking at those jeans across the court, how sure were you? I mean, really sure that they were fake?"

It seemed to take forever. I knew how his mind worked. His answer this time would be rational. I looked up at the ceiling, gripped the receiver like a vice.

Please God, I thought, *give me a ninety percent or higher.*

"Eighty percent."

Not what I wanted to hear.

"And one final question, Lee."

"Yes."

"How sure are you that those jeans weren't yours? How sure are you they had never been in your apartment?"

"One hundred percent!"

"Lee, don't start that shit again, tell me I—"

"One hundred percent, babe. Those jeans weren't mine, I swear."

We talked for another five minutes. My mind was on another planet. I brought up the question of his DNA on the jeans.

"When I was arrested, they took a mouth swab and fingerprints, babe. It's routine these days. A clever, bent copper could easily get a little DNA on those jeans."

"But how?"

"I don't know, babe. I don't know the technicalities, but they did. Please, believe me, I swear on my mother's life, those jeans weren't mine."

I ended the call, said goodbye.

I telephoned Jeremy the next day; I told him I was ready to go ahead as soon as my pupillage was finished. Strangely enough, I'd slept well for a change and had a clear head. He countered me, asked me if I knew what I was doing and said that my reputation as a barrister could be ruined before it even started, and that worried me.

"I believe him, Jeremy, I have to do it."

"It's not a question of believing, it's a question of proving his innocence and, from where I'm standing, you won't know that until you are standing in court with those jeans in your sweaty palms."

"I know, Jeremy, I know all that, but I also know that every man should have a right to prove his innocence. It's what our justice system is all about."

"And you're willing to stake your reputation on him?"

"I am. He's my husband, and even if there was just a squeak of a chance that I could get him out of there and back where he belongs, then I'd do it."

I heard a deep, frustrating sigh at the other end of the line, but Jeremy had sensed the determination in my voice. He knew I was ready to move hell and high water to take this into the Court of Appeal.

He said he'd ask for a new hearing date. He wished me luck and gave me a bit of a confidence boost when he said that if anyone could pull this off, then I was the person to do it.

36

HARD WORK AND APPLICATION

I'd read a quote somewhere from an American sportsman that I'd never heard of. It was something along the lines that the dictionary is the only place where success comes before work. Work comes before success every other time. Hard work and application. My mantra. It was something I always tried to follow and the reason I'd been successful in my Law exams.

But this was different because I believed I had everything I needed. Or rather, I had very little. We were clinging to the hope that the jeans the police had presented would be fake, and furthermore that I could prove it once I was in court.

The appeal was adjourned for several months but I didn't want to lose the momentum and I started writing my skeleton argument for the judge, the argument I would present in the Court of Appeal. Jeremy said that the police would likely be there, just to keep an eye on things. They had convicted Lee on circumstantial evidence and had been rewarded with a prison sentence. It was my job to show to the judge that the evidence was flawed, gain a retrial or even an immediate release.

My heart wasn't in it and, after less than an hour, I got up from the computer and walked into the kitchen.

Jeremy had burst my bubble when he had produced the three pairs of jeans. And while I had cursed him all the way home, he had only been doing his job and perhaps made me prepare a little more. I wouldn't be walking into the appeal so confidently; perhaps that was a good thing.

I made a cup of coffee and carried it back to the computer. I logged onto Google, determined to make myself feel better. I knew that DI David Graham had handled the Asprey armed robbery so, out of curiosity, I keyed in his name, rank and associated police station. He appeared in more than thirty results, named as the detective responsible for a particular conviction and a hardened criminal banged to rights somewhere within the Met's jurisdiction. Two commendations for bravery were mentioned. There were several photos of him, a video on YouTube outside a court somewhere, giving a press conference stating that he was happy with the conviction of a man called Gerhard Spreakson.

Another video of Graham, this time presenting a cheque to a children's charity, a generous donation from the Freemasons. So, Graham was a Freemason, nothing unusual about that. I'd heard that half the police force were in the Masons. He was also a family man. More digging around the internet brought up his wife's name and her Facebook page and her profile was public so without even 'friending' her, I checked out her pictures. She was nice, her twin sons cute and her daughter, angelic-looking. Him… he looked the odd man out in photos: sullen, grey looking, stone-faced.

I looked closely at the photos and decided I didn't like him; I was ready to do battle. His wife and kids? I decided I liked what I saw but tried not to think about them. If I proved that the jeans the police had shown were fake and I got Lee's conviction overturned, the detective's career would be ruined, the jeans, an obvious plant. That's what I would be saying, accusing our dear old boys in blue of dishonesty and underhand tactics.

I'd been on the computer for over two hours when I thought I'd search the unusual name. Gerhard, surely someone with a little German blood in his veins?

Gerhard Spreakson was a convicted armed robber, seems like this crime was Graham's speciality. Spreakson had a bag load of form ever since his teenage years, burglary, a couple of muggings, assault and GBH. He was bad news, the type of man who was better behind bars than he was roaming the streets of the capital. And then my eye caught another search headline. 'Gerhard Spreakson Loses Appeal.'

I clicked and read the feature, just six paragraphs reported by the *Daily Telegraph*. Spreakson's case had been heard by Judge Terence Keegan, who had declared that Graham's failure to disclose crucial evidence had been wholly wrong. He was quoted as saying, 'The failure to disclose this evidence has been accepted by the Crown and what happened should not have happened.' It didn't say what the evidence was. Judge Keegan also said that it was a 'serious and surprising mistake by a respected and long-serving policeman'. The court acknowledged that the officers involved should have known better and had made a serious error of judgment.

I was amazed as I read on.

'Despite acknowledging the problems with this evidence, the Court of Appeal declined to quash Spreakson's conviction.'

I couldn't believe what I was reading and the worst probable scenario infiltrated my mind. What if those jeans were fake? What if I could prove beyond all doubt that the only piece of evidence the police had was a sham? The final decision was still up to the judge and, in order for the judge to quash Lee's conviction, he would be openly admitting that a policeman with commendations of bravery and a long, distinguished service record, had been complicit in activities that were unlawful. What were the chances of that?

After another sleepless night, I was at Jeremy's office first thing. Luckily, he had no appointments until midday and he agreed to see me. As soon as I sat down, he knew something was wrong.

"What's up? You look like shit," he remarked.

"I haven't slept; it was something I read online yesterday."

I slid the article across the table. "Are you familiar with this case?"

He looked down and read a few lines. "Yes, Spreakson still lost his appeal, despite the police withholding vital evidence."

"Can that happen?"

"It has happened." He stabbed a finger on the desk. "There's your proof. It's rare, thank God, but the judge still believed that there wasn't enough to release Spreakson."

"But that's not right; the police had withheld vital evidence. That evidence may have resulted in not guilty at the trial."

Jeremy shrugged his shoulders. "The judge didn't think so."

"My God, this is so frustrating. Even if we get a result on the jeans, the judge could still find against us."

"That's the risk you agreed to take, Cookie. I warned you."

Before I could answer, he'd tilted the screen of his PC so that we could both see it, already typing into Google search.

"Here," he said. "Another famous loss at the Court of Appeal, the defence barrister, thought she had it all cut and dried." He pointed to the name of the prisoner. "She tore the evidence to shreds, but the judge still quashed the appeal."

"Look what the barrister said afterwards."

I couldn't bear to look at the screen. Jeremy read it out and as each sentence registered, I felt my blood turning to ice.

"She said, 'Miscarriages of justice don't just happen in the trial courts. Today, a miscarriage of justice happened in the Court of Appeal. The judge gave a judgment, which quite frankly shows how broken the criminal appeal system is in this country.'"

"Shit, she didn't hold back, did she?"

Jeremy continued. "She said it wasn't disputed that the police and prosecutors had failed to hand over crucial evidence to the defence during the original trial. She claimed she had presented and proved this beyond doubt. She said it was a dark and bitter day for British Justice."

Jeremy stood. He started his little pacing routine around the desk. "You have to remember that these judges on the circuit all look out for each other. If the judges in these two cases found for the defendant, then they are effectively telling the world that the judge at the original trial fucked up."

"Is that a legal term?"

Jeremy smiled. "It is. But the only problem is that these judges don't like to admit that their old chums have fucked up."

I sat for another ten minutes while Jeremy took me through another three cases, where circumstantial evidence was proven to be unstable and yet the appeals weren't still quashed.

"And your case is worse, Cookie, because even if you can prove that the jeans were fake the judge at the Court of Appeal will not only be telling the world that the original judge fucked up, but that the police have planted evidence to boot."

"So, I'm fucked. Is that what you are saying?"

Jeremy slid back in his seat. "There was a very good reason I didn't take the case."

He fiddled with a pen on the desk, doodled on a desk pad. "You need to look harder; you need more. You need to somehow prove that those jeans were never worn by Lee and that there was no way they could have been at the robbery."

"And how the hell am I going to do that?"

On his feet again. "I don't know, Cookie, I'm a busy man, I haven't looked into it, that's your job."

Jeremy walked to the door and opened it. He looked at his watch. I'd used up enough of his time. I was on my own. I thanked him and set off along the corridor.

"Take a look at the gunshot residue, Cookie," he said before closing the door.

Why had he said that? I'd referred to gunshot residue in my grounds of appeal, yet had more or less totally ignored it since focusing wholly and solely on those bloody fake jeans. The forensic report from the lab man from Birmingham had been requested by Jeremy and a copy lay on my desk. The original defence barrister had questioned none of it. I don't think he'd even read it through. I would start there.

37

COURT OF APPEAL

Six months passed quickly, and I now had Rights of Audience in any court, including the High Court. It was D Day, decision day, and I was all alone. If this all fell apart, I would have wondered about my mental health. It was something Jeremy had said; something about my career being over before it had even begun. It was black and white, open and shut, there was nothing in between. Whatever happened at the end of this momentous day would be down to me.

Lee would be there of course, but he'd be nothing more than a spectator, there were no plans to question him, but I intended to put Professor Tremlett on the stand even though I knew it was highly irregular and wasn't even sure that the judge would allow it. I had requested his presence and, of course, I'd asked for those jeans to be present in court. I travelled in on the bus, a stop-start journey of nearly an hour, which gave me more time to plan the rest of my presentation.

Judge Purvis was a dour man; bespectacled with a long full wig, nearer eighty than he was seventy with a bulbous red nose. It was just after ten in the morning when we started, and I figured we would need to get this wrapped up fairly quickly. The judge looked the type who enjoyed long, hydraulic lunches with an equally long post-lunch nap afterwards.

We waited until Lee was escorted in. He was in handcuffs; four burly prison officers accompanied him and they sat him behind a bulletproof screen with two uniformed, armed police sitting down below. It was way over the top, but I had expected it. Already they were sewing the guilty seeds in the judge's mind, the big, dangerous black man, the vicious armed robber who should be locked up for life; the keys thrown in the Thames.

The prosecution barrister, Clive Watson, was up first. He started with the CCTV footage from the jewellers, made a point of freezing the footage on the armed robber, casting deliberate glances towards Lee in the dock. The inference was obvious. He said that Lee's name had been passed to the police from the criminal underworld. He didn't mention a snitch, of course, but said it was common knowledge and that the stolen watches from Asprey's had been distributed around the capital by Lee. There was no actual proof of this, of course, and it was something that hadn't even been mentioned at the first trial. He'd thrown it into the mix with a bonus for the judge and, if I'd been allowed to object, I'd have jumped up like a shot.

But not in the Court of Appeal in the Royal Courts of Justice, the second most senior court in England and Wales.

The barrister had a wooden cane in his right hand. He'd frozen the footage and was pointing at the jeans, the white Stone Island patch. He referred to the cost and how expensive they were and that they weren't worn by the average man in the street. I allowed myself a slight smile of satisfaction. The footage hadn't been enhanced; it was the poor CCTV video from the shop.

He switched the projector off. I noticed a casual glance toward Graham, who nodded ever so slightly. Smug bastards. The barrister moved swiftly onto the forensic report, touched on the DNA and then the gunshot residue. And then he sat down. I couldn't believe it.

I checked my watch. Twelve minutes, forty-one seconds. What was he playing at? I had timed my appeal at well over an hour. And then it came to me. It was my first trial in front of a proper judge; I'd only recently finished pupillage. I was a junior, a rookie. What sort of damage could I do?

"Miss Walker."

The judge's voice brought me back from my thoughts.

"Miss Walker, I realise you are new to this court, but it's your turn to speak now."

A couple of laughs. Someone cleared their throat, as I got to my feet, trembling. It felt like my knees were going to buckle. I steadied myself, adjusting my robe as I took my position in front of the lectern. The adrenalin kicked in and a strange calm washed over me. I deserved to be here, I'd worked my arse off and the man I loved sat only a matter of yards away, chained up like a wild animal.

I vowed that, by the end of the day, those chains would be removed and he'd be coming home with me because I was going to prove that those jeans were not only fake but planted by a bent cop. The jeans were in a polythene bag on a table by the judge. The prosecution barrister hadn't bothered with them, hadn't removed them from the bag.

"My Lord," I said, "as you know, the appellant was convicted on just one piece of circumstantial evidence, namely," I pointed at the table, "those jeans which were allegedly recovered during a second police raid on the appellant's flat. The prosecution alleged that the jeans were rare, that they were expensive and that they were the same pair of jeans that the armed robber wore during the raid on Asprey Jewellers. Those jeans that sit on the table are the key to the appellant spending the next ten years of his life in prison. The appellant, My Lord, an innocent man, will be robbed of the opportunity to see his sons grow into young men. His boys are suffering; they miss him every day, so it's not just Mr Corey who is paying for this dreadful miscarriage of justice."

I laid it on thick. I painted the picture of innocence, of a hard-working family man with a son and step-son, and wondered how much the judge knew about Lee's criminal past. I spoke longer than Mr Watson, the prosecution barrister had for the duration of his appeal submission and then I started on the real nitty-gritty.

I asked the court clerk to remove the jeans from the plastic evidence bag. I had a magnifying glass in my pocket for the judge. He would need to look at the rivets, to see that there was no Stone Island engraving and when I had shown him that, I could bring in my CCTV footage.

But I could see the rivets were engraved. There would be no need for the magnifying glass.

I swear my heart stopped. I switched tactic.

"The gunshot residue," I said. "It's not exactly reliable evidence, is it?"

Our forensic man from Birmingham wriggled uncomfortably in his seat.

"With your permission, My Lord, I'd like to question Professor Tremlett on certain aspects of his report."

The prosecution barrister jumped to his feet and objected as I knew he would. He said that an appeal court was not the place to question independent experts.

"I am well aware of that," I told the judge. "However, the original defence barrister didn't raise any questions relating to the professor's report and I think he should have."

"Be my guest," the judge said. "Professor, would you like to take the stand, please?"

The professor stood, walked over to witness box by the judge and sat down. The court clerk handed him a copy of his own report and gave one to the judge.

"Professor," I said. "Would you say that gunshot residue is one of your areas of speciality?"

He glared at me as he spoke. I knew that I was in for a fight. "Not really. Our laboratory deals with all kinds of forensics, including DNA."

"Yes," I quickly glanced at the front page of his report in my hand, "I see that, but just let us concentrate on the gunshot residue for a minute. We both know how gunshot residue can find its way onto the clothing and the skin of someone who pulls the trigger of a pistol or a shotgun."

"Yes, we do."

"Can you explain that to the judge, please?"

The professor turned ever so slightly in his seat. "Well, My Lord, when the firing pin strikes the primer and detonates, the propellant ignites and the round is forced down the chamber and out of the barrel. When the round exits the barrel, the gases escape through various openings in the gun, some of which condense and generate particles. It's unavoidable that some of these particles will be deposited on the person doing the shooting and, in some cases, people who are also standing in close proximity to the shooter."

"Good," I nodded in agreement. "And professor, would you say that the evidence of gunshot residue is reliable?" before he could answer, I continued, "because I've become a bit of an expert on gunshot residue too. I've studied no less than eleven criminal cases where gunshot residue has produced what is known as false positives, and that evidence has been thrown out completely."

The judge looked at the professor over the top of his glasses, coughed and cleared his throat. "Can you explain what Miss Walker is talking about? In layman's terms, please."

"Yes, My Lord, Miss Walker is referring to the cases of—"

I jumped in immediately. "The cases of the Crown verses, Bridgewater, Smailes, Graham, Ashcroft, Knowles, Smith and Persimon, Gates, Rostock, Hammond, Mosher and McKintosh."

That took the bastards by surprise, I thought. *The rookie had done her homework.*

"Yes, I know of some of those cases. I think she is referring to the samples that can be found from certain occupations like welding, people who cut keys, mechanics, and people who work with certain paper products. It has been suggested that there are a dozen or so professions which can produce false positives for gunshot residue."

"I see," said the judge. "So gunshot residue forensics doesn't necessarily guarantee that it came from a gunshot."

"Not in some cases, My Lord, but in this particular case I'm reasonably confident that there were enough particles to constitute residue from a gunshot."

"Really?" I questioned as I raised the report to eye level. "And do you know Mr Corey's occupation?"

"I don't."

"Then how can you be so sure?"

He stalled for a second or two. The professor looked over towards Graham who offered nothing in return.

"How do you know that Mr Corey isn't a mechanic, for example?"

"I don't," he answered quickly, "that's not what I was asked to do, but I stand firm on my report, that I believe it was gunshot residue on those jeans."

"I see."

I'd planted just one seed of doubt. Keep sowing.

"There's something else that worries me about your report, professor, the absence of low copy DNA."

The professor said nothing.

I turned over to the last page of the report and turned to the judge. "On page four, My Lord, you see at the bottom of the page there is a section relating to low copy DNA. A table. Low copy DNA found on clothing can be retrieved from tiny particles of skin not visible to the human eye. We see on page three, on a similar table, that a significant DNA particle was found on the jeans, namely a pubic hair." I pointed to Lee behind the screen. "That man's pubic hair." I turned to the professor. "A perfect match, I believe, professor."

"Yes, a one hundred percent match."

"Which would indicate that the jeans had been worn by the appellant, am I right?"

"Yes," said the professor.

I paused for a moment, looked at the judge and then back at the professor. "But no low copy DNA, no skin particles were found anywhere on the jeans, professor?"

"No. no low copy DNA.

"Just the pubic hair."

"Yes."

"Which is why it puzzles me, because if a pair of jeans had been worn by the prisoner, I would have expected at least a little level of low copy DNA to have been found, wouldn't you?"

"Yes and no. If the jeans were relatively new or they had been recently washed, you wouldn't necessarily find any low copy DNA."

"And yet you'd find normal levels of DNA, like a pubic hair?"

"It's possible."

"But not probable."

The professor looked at the judge. He wanted to be rescued. I had sown seed number two.

"It's a nonsense, My Lord, those jeans over there are brand new, they've never been worn, not by the appellant or anyone else and they certainly have been nowhere near Asprey Jewellers. They were the only piece of evidence the police presented, the reason the appellant is currently in prison and quite frankly, this evidence should have been thrown out at the original trial. I don't know how they ever ended up in the appellant's flat, but it's quite remarkable how they were overlooked during the first raid."

The judge looked at me sternly over his bifocals. "Miss Walker up to this point I have made allowances due to your inexperience in this court, but if I think you're suggesting that a decorated police officer has been complicit in planting false evidence, then you are treading on thin ice."

"My Lord, I'm not suggesting that for a second, I'm merely presenting the facts. It is for you, My Lord, to pull the facts together and come to your own conclusion, but if I may, My Lord, there is another point I need to address you on."

"Yes... " he said in the drawn-out way that only Appeal Court Judges can, looking annoyed but intrigued at the same time.

"And to make this point I need to ask the professor one further question"

"Miss Walker, is this really necessary?"

"I apologise, My Lord, but I'm new to this as you know."

"I know, but—"

"Please, My Lord, just one final question."

The judge let out a deliberate long sigh, gazed up at the ceiling. "This is highly unconventional, Miss Walker; you've been on your feet nearly an hour. Mr Watson took less than fifteen minutes. Is this point in your grounds of appeal?

"Yes, My Lord."

"Well, okay then, if you must."

"I must."

The professor sat patiently; he had clearly heard my discussion with the judge.

It wasn't so much a question I had for him though, more a statement of fact.

"Professor, turning back to gunshot residue. Do you know how long it stays detectable under normal circumstances?"

"Not really," he answered. "There's a lot of differing opinions among forensic experts."

"Take an estimated guess," I said.

"I don't guess. I found gunshot residue on the jeans and whether it had been there two hours or two weeks, it would have made no difference to the report I was asked to compile."

"But you are aware that the residue has a limited lifespan, which starts to fade just a few hours after the firearm discharge?"

"Yes."

I pulled out three copies of the report I had printed. I handed one to my learned friend, Mr Watson, one to the judge and one to the professor. "This is a gunshot residue report by the number one recognised expert on gunshot residue in the United States, a forensic expert called William Patterson, the so-called God of gunshot residue."

I drew their attention to page two, halfway down where I had highlighted with yellow highlighter, 'gunshot residue exists up to 5.27 days after a firearm discharge.'

"Five point two seven days. I don't think we could get any more specific than that," I said.

The judge frowned. "Just tell me the significance of the report, Miss Walker; I'm not here to play games."

"It's very simple, My Lord, the armed robbery on Asprey's was carried out on the seventh of March, and according to the professor's report, he carried out the test on the jeans on the fifteenth of July. Wherever that gunshot residue came from, it did not come from the armed robbery on Asprey Jewellers."

My final sentence stirred up a bit of a hornet's nest.

Watson stood up in a fury, his face like thunder. "This is highly irregular, My Lord," he spluttered, struggling to get his words out quickly enough. I sat back in my seat and watched the fun. Mr Watson was complaining about the flexibility afforded to me by the judge. He said that I had been taking liberties playing on the fact that it was my first appearance in court. The judge rose and announced a thirty-minute adjournment exiting quickly from the courtroom. Watson and Graham disappeared out the door in a hurried rush, whispering as they squeezed through the heavy double doors, followed slowly by the professor, who didn't really know what he should or should not be doing. All of my confidence drained away. I was on my own again. I looked over to Lee and he mouthed, 'What's up?'

I looked down at the floor and covered my face with my hands. I was getting stitched up, that's what was happening, and I thought of the female barrister Jeremy had mentioned on my last visit to his office that the Court of Appeal's system was broken.

38

THIRTY MINUTES

Thirty minutes seemed like an hour. But I put the time to good use. I suspected there may be some serious discussions going on in the corridors or the conference rooms of the Court of Appeal that day, and I knew it was all down to me.

Jeremy had warned me to prepare a plan B, and that's exactly what I had put in place. But had I worried one man enough to convince him that Lee's conviction was flawed, based on one piece of circumstantial evidence that the boys in blue had planted?

Unlikely, I thought.

It was Graham who walked in first. He gave me a sly glance and I could tell from his body language that things had gone according to plan. He looked a little sheepish though. He'd been giving a good dressing down, definitely screwed up somewhere along the way. His gunshot evidence was seriously flawed and, because the five to six day forensic longevity was accepted by most experts, in his desperation to frame my husband, he had fucked that up.

I knew why; the entire process had taken four months. To begin with, they hadn't a clue who the robbers were so, by the time they'd raided Lee's flat and waited for the forensic reports on the first set of clothing, the clock was ticking. When the results had come back negative, he had another bite at the cherry, saying they had found the Stone Island jeans. This time he thought he had made sure that the cherry was sweet, but the time lapse didn't tie in with fresh gunshot residue.

The professor from Birmingham was next. He walked into the court in his bespoke, tailor-made suit, with his head held high. He'd done nothing wrong of course, he was quite professional and to be fair to him, he hadn't bent a single rule. His report was accurate and, after all, his fee had been paid by the police, so of course he was going to side with them.

I was safe in the knowledge that he hadn't known anything about the jeans being planted, and his report on the low copy DNA was spot on. It was just a crying shame that the original barrister hadn't picked up on it at the time.

Mr Watson came in last and didn't look at me.

Then Judge Purvis walked in and the court rose whilst he took his seat. He had a word with the court clerk and she took some notes from him. We all waited. I looked over at Lee. He knew. He couldn't look me in the eye; he knew he was going downstairs again.

The Right Honourable Judge John Purvis QC began his summing up. He started by saying that he had been more than impressed by Counsel for the Appellant. He said I'd handled my first case with enviable professionalism, and at times he found it difficult to believe that he wasn't dealing with a barrister with decades more experience.

The patronising fuck, I thought.

I knew what was coming.

"Whilst we must respect the five-point two seven-day gunshot residue theory from our friend in the US, as Professor Tremlett explained to me, there are a lot of different opinions as to how long gunshot residue hangs around after a gun discharge."

Bullshit, I thought again.

"I note that I asked Professor Tremlett about aspects of the DNA results and whether low copy DNA could be removed during a normal washing machine cycle. He said it was unlikely, but didn't feel he was in a position to speculate that this would be the case. It would depend on the temperature of the wash, the duration of the washing cycle and the strength of the detergent. As far as we are aware, this has never been tested and therefore, unless it can be proved otherwise, we must assume that the absence of low copy DNA is down to the fact that the jeans had been thoroughly cleaned prior to them being found at the appellant's property."

More bullshit, I thought, yet again.

The judge looked at me directly. "Miss Walker, while you don't want to hear this, I'm afraid that you haven't presented me with sufficient new evidence to convince me that the jeans presented at the original trial, the jeans we see over there today, the very jeans that Professor Tremlett analysed forensically, are different to that which we saw the armed robber wearing at the scene of the robbery. Furthermore, a majority jury also believed at the time that the two pairs of jeans were one and the same item. Nothing that I have been presented with today can convince me to change my mind. For me, there are just too many coincidences. The make of the jeans, the DNA, the gunshot residue. It all adds up."

He cleared his throat and continued, this time staring Lee in the face. "Lee Corey, I—"

I stood up. "I haven't finished, My Lord."

He glared at me. "What do you mean you haven't finished?" he boomed.

"I mean, My Lord, I haven't finished addressing you on all the points raised in my Grounds of Appeal. You cut me short when you rose to take a thirty-minute break, the adjournment."

"I... I... but I thought you'd finished."

"Then you were wrong, My Lord."

The judge looked at the court clerk and then over at Mr Watson.

"I am entitled to read my Grounds of Appeal in full," I said, "and you haven't allowed me to do that."

He called over the court clerk. They exchanged a few whispers. He then turned back to me.

"How long will this take, Miss Walker?"

"As long as necessary, My Lord."

He looked at his watch, grimaced, and then waved his hand in a circular motion, urging me to continue. He was ready for his liquid lunch. The beads of sweat and a slight trembling of his hands gave the game away.

I asked the court clerk to turn on the projector.

During the recess, I had inserted my enhanced footage of the CCTV tape and ran it through to where the armed robber storms into the shop. I explained how I'd had the video enhanced by a professional company specialising in CCTV graphics. I looked over towards Graham. His face was the colour of a Royal Navy frigate on a dark, Portsmouth morning.

I had the remote control in my hand and I pressed play; I allowed only thirty seconds and then pressed pause at the time the gunman turned to face the camera head-on. I took up the story. I was enjoying every delicious second.

"My Lord, you have said on no fewer than four occasions today, that you believed that the reason the appellant was convicted for the armed robbery on Asprey's, was because of the belief that the jeans you see in this video and the jeans presented to this court," I pointed to the jeans, "were one and the same item. I concur with you one hundred percent and I've said on more than one occasion today that it was the sole reason the appellant was convicted. My learned friend, Mr Watson, has laboured that point too on numerous occasions, and at the original trial, DI Graham apologised to the jury for offering nothing more than this one pair of jeans. There was no other evidence found, no ID parade, no fingerprints or DNA at the scene, no stolen items recovered that could be traced back directly to the appellant and the firearm used in the raid has still not been recovered. In a nutshell, My Lord, those jeans on the table were all the prosecution had and if they couldn't link those jeans to the crime scene, then they had nothing."

The silence was deafening. You could have heard a pin drop as I fingered the remote control and zoomed in on the jeans a little more.

"The jeans the armed robber wore on the day of the robbery were Stone Island jeans, I don't dispute that and nor do I dispute they would undoubtedly have had gunshot residue on them at one point and also low copy DNA, even if they had been washed a dozen times. You see, My Lord, human skin is an incredible organ, the human body is made up of around ten trillion cells in total. Your skin makes up fifteen percent of your body weight, which equates to approximately one and a half trillion skin cells. Over a twenty-four-hour period, we lose almost a million skin cells. So to suggest that a hot wash can eradicate a million cells is, quite frankly, nonsense because those cells get everywhere, in every nook and cranny, in pockets, in seams, in zips and in button holes."

The professor's gaze dropped to the floor.

I turned my attention to the projector again, zoomed in a little more. "It's the attention to detail on things like the pockets and the rivets on the pockets which proved to me beyond doubt that there are clearly two pairs of jeans. Look on the left-hand side of the front left pocket gentlemen. Look, there's a knife pocket. You can just about see it. In the old days of the Wild West and the often deadly saloon brawls, many establishments made the cowboys leave their weapons at the door. The knife pocket was a pocket inside a pocket, a secret way to conceal a small weapon, always on the left-hand side of the jeans because most of the cowboys were right-handed."

I looked towards Graham. "Don't you just love a little history?"

"Get on with it," the judge barked. "We haven't got all day."

I apologised and continued. I zoomed right in on one of the knife pocket rivets.

"Let's concentrate on the rivets of these jeans."

The rivet filled the whole screen and as clear as day, the Stone Island, engraved cross.

I looked across to Graham again. There was a little more colour in his cheeks now, because he too had checked the rivets on the dodgy jeans he'd bought from the market and he was confident that his copier had cut no corners, that they were engraved with the Stone Island cross.

"Perhaps DI Graham can be permitted to inspect his jeans for the court." The judge nodded. The court clerk carefully picked up the jeans and handed them to the policeman. "Tell the judge what you see, detective, paying close attention to the rivets."

Graham inspected the jeans. He checked the white patch and the rivets on the front and back pockets.

"Well, detective?"

He looked over at the judge. "May I speak, My Lord?"

"Please do, the judge answered back." Another glance at his watch and a shake of his head.

He stood up. He held out the jeans with both hands. "I see an identical pair of jeans to that which the barrister has just shown us in her CCTV footage. That's what I see, sir, the very same jeans that Professor Tremlett analysed; the jeans I personally recovered from her client's flat. The Stone Island cross is clearly visible on each rivet."

I paused again for dramatic effect. It was a game; a big act and I was ready for the closing scene.

"Identical, DI Graham?"

"Yes."

"Are you absolutely sure?"

"I've never been more certain of anything in my twenty-five years of service to the public."

"The knife pocket," I said. "Would you say the knife pocket was identical too?"

He looked down. Turned the jeans over. I saw him scan the front. His fingers prised the front left pocket apart. He searched desperately for the knife pocket.

"You won't find it, detective," I said. "You won't find it because it isn't there; the copiers decided it wasn't worth the trouble."

I placed both hands on the lectern in front of me for maximum effect. "The jeans you are holding in your sweaty little palms were planted in the appellant's property weren't they Detective Graham, they were planted with gunshot residue already attached and then dragged through the sheets on his bed because you were safe in the knowledge that they would pick up a trace of his DNA. Isn't that right? They were never worn by the appellant, and they were never worn by the armed robber either."

That's when the shit hit the fan.

The judge picked up his gavel and banged it hard on its block on the bench, shouting, "Order, order in the court!"

He looked at me and gave me the biggest dressing down I had ever had, saying I had broken every rule in the book and if he ever saw me in his court again, it would be too soon.

39

TYING UP LOOSE ENDS

The obscure, but nevertheless, genius criminologist, Frederick Dempsey, once said during a lecture at Yale University, that even the cleverest criminal will make at least three mistakes appertaining to his or her crime. Dempsey focused on homicide. More often than not, they pulled him into cases where it was suspected that a serial killer was on the loose.

Dempsey said that the average serial killer was smart, that a lot of planning went into each murder, but before, during, and after the crime, at least one mistake would be made at each juncture. He called it 'the three-stage meltdown' and it was up to the detectives to find those mistakes.

The clues were there if you looked hard enough and long enough and generally, just the one mistake would be enough to catch the killer and get a conviction.

Throughout history, killers have been caught this way. He detailed the dozens of murderers who had been caught by the morbid fascination of wanting to return to the scene of the crime, how some had even attended the funerals of some of their victims. The 'afterburner' he called it.

In an online article, Dempsey told how the patience of the Los Angeles police, in the case of Geovanni Borjas, eventually paid off. They had no suspect in the brutal 2011 murders of twenty-two-year-old Bree'Anza Guzman and seventeen-year-old Michelle Lozano, both murdered after being raped.

Both crime scenes were clean as a whistle, without any meaningful clues. They didn't have a suspect. A few names were banded around the criminal circuit, but Geovanni Borjas's name was not one of them. He had made no mistakes pre or post-crime; no boasts to his friends or associates during a drunken rant or a drug-induced high. Borjas was clean, not even a minor offence committed in his teen years.

Years passed, but the detectives kept to their task and, as detection of DNA methods improved, they could retrieve a tiny piece of DNA from the scene. They ran the DNA through police databases and Borjas's father, who had once been arrested on a domestic violence charge, came up as a likely close relative of the killer. The match wasn't identical, but the detectives knew that there was a real possibility that a son or possibly a brother may be responsible for the murders of the two women.

Police needed an exact match, but there was nothing on the database for Borjas and because there wasn't a single scrap of evidence, they couldn't bring him in. So, they tailed Geovanni Borjas for several days and then they saw him spit on the ground. The police sprang into action, gathered up his saliva, and found an exact DNA match. It had taken nearly six years before Geovanni Borjas had made his mistake, but Dempsey said it always happened and commended the detectives.

In the same article, Dempsey also alluded to the bizarre notion that some criminals even left behind deliberate clues at the scene of the crime. This aspect of the criminal's mind fascinated me. From Jack the Ripper to the Zodiac Killer, criminals love to taunt the police and there are many incidents of murderers writing to newspapers or even radio and television stations.

I knew Lee was guilty.

I'd known ever since the day I had asked him about his percentages relating to the fake jeans and how sure he was that the jeans the police had presented in court had belonged to him.

He'd said he was eighty percent sure that the jeans were copied. The figure had been disappointing to me initially. He was effectively telling me he didn't know, there was a definite doubt there. But when I asked him how sure he was that the jeans weren't his, he jumped in immediately, without a second thought, and said, "One hundred percent."

There was only one reason he had said that, because he had disposed of every pair of Stone Island jeans, he possessed, and more importantly, the exact pair of jeans that he'd worn during the robbery, the jeans that would have linked him to the crime scene. While he had favoured Evisu and Armani of late, he certainly wouldn't have given away or disposed of his beloved branded jeans for no good reason.

But he did. He either dumped them or burned them because he knew he'd fucked up. What sort of idiot would take part in an armed robbery wearing Stone Island jeans in a store that had CCTV security cameras? It was Dempsey's middle section of the three-stage meltdown. Lee had also made a second mistake in that jewellery store.

The first part of Dempsey's meltdown, the 'before crime' mistake, had taken shape over many years. When the CIA recruits their personnel, the number one requirement is that the candidate must be non-descript. They must not stand out in a crowd. It's not exactly good practice that a spy walks into a room and everyone sits up and takes notice. No. You'll find that the average CIA agent is about as non-descript as you could imagine. You won't notice them, they'll have been and gone before anyone even realises.

I had to meet a CIA man at Heathrow Airport one day. He was giving evidence in a case that my firm was working on and, as General Counsel, it was my job to go to the airport to meet him.

I stood at the arrivals gate with a sign that read *James McVicar*. (Not his real name.) I watched and waited. I was trying to see if I could pick my man out, carefully studying men of a certain type as they walked through the gates. I don't know what I was expecting, but a pre-conceived notion of a certain type, perhaps a big muscly bloke in a sharp suit, late twenties, early thirties, a big white smile for sure, and sunglasses.

The man who tapped me on the shoulder looked like an elderly baggage handler. Only the baggage handlers were better dressed. He was nearing sixty years of age, wispy thinning hair, a hooked nose and built like he had been starved in a concentration camp for a few years. Non-descript.

If I'd had to pick him out in an ID parade a month or two later, I would have struggled, and that, he explained in the car, was the whole point. Lee was the total opposite of non-descript and believe me, it's not the look a professional criminal should go for.

Lee was big and brash, he was loud, good looking, he wore designer clothes and fancy watches, Lee had a different watch for every day of the week, not one of them cost less than five grand. Lee walked into a room and everyone stared. He rubbed some men up the wrong way; the girls fell at his feet and more often than not, made a pass at him; they couldn't wait to drag him into bed.

That didn't go down too well with his male counterparts and Lee had made a lot of enemies on the street and with the police, you could say he could get away with murder and most of the time, he came out on top.

It wasn't so much a single mistake that he'd made before the crime, just something that had festered for a long time and, given the opportunity, the average police informant wouldn't think twice about dropping the name of Corey into a conversation. In fact, most of them would be pretty damned pleased to do so, to get him out of the streets and into jail.

Then there was Lee's post-crime mistake.

He thought he was being clever, lying low for a few months, and clearly that was the sensible thing to do. Flooding the black market with expensive watches a few weeks after a major armed robbery was the easiest way to bring the cops knocking on your door. Clever Lee, or Cooper, as he was nicknamed by a select few of his mates. Or so he thought.

But a few months wasn't long enough. He should have waited at least a year or even two. But he figured it was time to turn in a profit. It was too soon and he also made the fatal error of handling the watches himself. Lee wanted maximum return from the raid and was not about to cut into the profits using more middle-men than were necessary, nor was he prepared to jump in a car and travel to Scotland or Ireland or even further afield.

Mistake after mistake after mistake.

Lee shit on his own doorstep and moved the watches himself in London. It was a monumental mistake, unforgiveable. And the London fence, Jackson, known as The Watch Man, had given Lee's name up to Graham.

The police took one of the watches Lee had given to The Watch Man, and Asprey Jewellers confirmed it was a marked, limited edition, one of only 500 that had come from their shop; it was one of the items stolen in the raid.

The snitch had come good, and the police knew they had their man. Now it was just a case of proving it. If they couldn't prove it legitimately, then they'd find a way. Their informant was deep undercover, and they knew he couldn't testify in court that the watch had come from Lee, so they had to work on something else. The Stone Island jeans.

Lee had made many mistakes, both pre and post-crime and two big whoppers, slap bang in between. The police had found one, but it took a lot of hours on the enhanced CCTV footage before I found the other.

* * *

It was the day after I had successfully cleared his name in the Court of Appeal. He was a free man. Lee had gone out with his mates to celebrate. He asked me along, but I told him I was totally drained and that I needed to get an early night to recharge my batteries.

I'd spent hours going over that footage and although I'd been able to prove to a judge that the two pairs of jeans were not the same, I'd always felt that there was something else that both me and the police had missed.

I'd pulled the little magnifying glass icon over every single fibre on those jeans, studied every aspect of them, and then studied the gun, the bomber jacket, the sweatshirt and even the balaclava. It hadn't dawned on me to look at anything else, but it was something Jeremy had said about the possibility of the armed robber wearing cowboy boots.

So, as Lee basked in the adulation of freedom, accepted the handshakes, the fist pumps, the back slaps and everything that was dished out in a fancy wine bar in Kensington, I booted up the computer and slipped in the DVD to the drive.

I didn't need to wait long, just a couple of minutes in, and there it was, a full-length, back body shot from a camera at the front of the store. The magnifying glass instantly appeared on the screen when I pressed pause.

I dragged it down to Lee's feet. Yes, Lee's feet, because by now, I knew that the man in the balaclava pointing a pump-action shotgun at a terrified sales assistant was, in fact, my husband.

The heel of his right boot was exposed, four centimetres of a Cuban heeled boot, the sort of boots that Lee hated with a passion, but boots that would add a few inches to his height and if push came to shove, a good barrister could argue the point that the armed robber did not fit the profile of the accused man. Doubt. A little doubt filtering into the minds of the jurors.

Lee had it all worked out. He'd thought of everything, even planning for an arrest if the worst came to the worst.

Where had he got those boots from? Would he have been stupid enough to borrow them from his brother Vince?

The magnifying glass picked out a deep gouge in the heel of the right boot. It was only a third of a centimetre long, in the shape of a 'J' but quite distinctive.

I closed down the computer and went to bed.

While Lee slept off his hangover the following morning, I went round to his brother's flat.

He opened the door, and I walked in. He asked me if I wanted a coffee.

"No," I replied, "I just want to see your cowboy boots."

He must have thought I had taken leave of my senses but, after I repeated my request several times, he let out a long sigh and walked away. He returned with four pairs of boots and I found the 'J' on the heel of the boot of the third pair.

"Did you know?" I asked him.

He said he didn't know what I was talking about.

"Did Lee ever borrow these?"

"No," he said. "You know as well as I do, he hates them."

"He must have borrowed them at some time; he wore them for the robbery on Asprey's."

The colour drained from Vincent's face as he flopped onto the sofa. He told me that he had left them at Lee's flat for several months. We talked dates and concluded that Lee had returned the boots just a day or two after the robbery.

I explained the CCTV footage and told him what I had found, how Lee had got rid of every pair of Stone Island jeans he'd ever owned. Poor Vince; a nice kid, as honest as the day was long. He slumped down onto the settee, head in hands shaking his head. He was broken. Vince had never doubted his brother's innocence ever since he had been charged and convicted all those years ago.

He looked up at me, his face twisted in grief. "How long have you known?"

I explained the telephone conversation between myself and Lee and how the penny had dropped when I realised he had got rid of his Stone Island jeans.

"Only the police and the armed robber knew about those jeans at that point. He got rid of them immediately after the robbery, prior to the raid on his flat, probably at the same time he returned your boots."

"I don't believe it," Vince said. "I don't fucking believe it."

He got up, let out a deep sigh and looked at me; a puzzled frown crossed his face. "But you still went to the Court of Appeal and you won. Why did you go through with it if you knew he was guilty?"

That was a good question, one I'd asked myself a hundred times and even as I stood up in front of the judge, ready to read out my first statement, I'd had second thoughts, I was so close to telling him that there'd been a big mistake and that I was withdrawing the appeal.

"Curiosity," I said.

"Curiosity?"

"Yes. I was curious about those jeans the police had supplied, curious to find out if there really was a bent copper trying to frame him."

"But he was guilty. How can you frame a guilty man?"

I could see Vincent's point. But the Law was just a game at the end of the day. The police knew Lee was guilty, and it was their job to prove it and mine to disprove it, if that was at all possible.

"The detectives were lazy, Vince. They cut corners. There were plenty of real clues to be found, if only they had looked hard enough. But no, we had one bent copper who was fixated on the jeans and couldn't wait to tie up the case. I carried on with the appeal because it was more important to expose this bent copper. How many other cases has he set up with false evidence? How many innocent people has he put away over the years?"

Vince shook his head. "My brother has been one lucky bastard."

I explained they were already looking into several of DI Graham's previous cases, that he'd been suspended pending an official enquiry.

I took Vince up on his offer of a coffee; we sat at the kitchen table and chatted some more. Vince asked me if Lee knew that I knew; I told him he didn't.

"But you have to confront him; he's made a fool of you."

Vince was angry now. He said that my career could have been ruined and he had no right putting me in that situation.

"You have to tell him, Cookie."

"I know, I will. Just give me time."

Vince didn't know that I had everything planned. It would take a while and there was paperwork to sort out, but I was planning to get a divorce. The one thing that I demanded from my husband and the father of my child was honesty and trust. With Lee, I had neither.

"There's something else I spotted on the CCTV from the jewellers."

"What?"

"Well, you know, whenever Lee sees someone wearing a UCLA sweatshirt or T-shirt?"

"Yeah."

"What does he say?"

"He says it's his university, the University of Corey Lee from Acton."

"That's right, UCLA."

"And what about it?"

I let out an involuntary laugh. In truth, I didn't know whether to laugh or cry. "The cocky bastard wore a UCLA sweatshirt during the raid."

Vince's jaw fell open as he jumped up from his seat. He leaned forward and planted his palms on the table. "No way."

"Yes."

"What's that all about then?"

"It's what criminals do, their idea of fun, something to brag about years later. I'm guessing that UCLA sweatshirt went to the same place as his jeans, the balaclava and his black bomber jacket. He's probably burned the lot!"

I left a shell-shocked Vince after our 'reveal all' coffee morning.

As I closed the door behind me, I inhaled the cool morning air deep into my lungs. I felt a still quite calm within; it felt good to talk, and I felt a lot better, sharing what I knew with someone I could trust.

Time to move on.